NALZAMBOR
Key Location Guide

PROLOGUE

THE DRAYKIS. BIG. SILENT. DEADLY. Finnius the acolyte of Barnabus had never seen or imagined anything like them. Men, with dragon parts grafted onto their bodies by magi: scales, talons, and another one with wings. Not just any men, but fighting men, men of skill and cunning. And they had something cornered, a dragon of all things.

They'd trapped a yellow streak dragon inside the mouth of a large cave. It was bigger than any one man, slender and about fifteen feet in length. Its spiked tail whipped out like the head of a snake, taking out one draykis's legs. In an instant, the draykis was back on its feet, charging. The dragon breathed a plume of white ash, engulfing the dragon man. The draykis turned stiff as stone where he stood.

Whack!

A draykis caught the dragon across the nose with his club as another draykis jumped onto its neck. Only a fool would wrestle a dragon, but the draykis were unrelenting, fearless. The yellow streak dragon bit one on the arm, clawed another on the face, but he was young and confined to a tight space. The fourth draykis appeared, the one with dark wings and a red scaled face, swinging a club. As the dragon men held the yellow dragon down, the winged draykis beat it until it fought no more. Finnius had never seen men take a dragon so quickly before. Nor with such brutality, either.

"What would you have us do now, Acolyte Finnius?" the winged draykis said.

Finnius watched as the other two bound the defenseless dragon's mouth and wings. He could see the look in the dragon's eyes, drained, defeated. That look thrilled him as he walked over and stroked the dragon's dark yellow belly. *Quite the catch. Quite the catch, indeed. High Priestess Selene will be pleased with this one.*

"Fetch a cart while this one thaws," he said, pointing his finger at a draykis that was coated in white and perfectly stiff. "And don't touch him—"

At that moment, a draykis touched the coated draykis and started to freeze.

"Either!" Finnius grunted as he turned back towards the draykis leader. "Fetch the cart while we wait for them both to thaw out." He shook his head. "Did I tell any of you to touch one another? Hmm? Did I? No! You follow orders. Explicit orders. Now fetch that cart and the rest of the acolytes, Dragon Man."

"As you command," the Draykis said, ruffling his wings before heading outside of the cave.

"You," he pointed at the last one, "stay with the dragon. We cannot afford to lose our bait for capturing Nath Dragon."

CHAPTER 1

MORGDON. HOME OF THE DWARVES. I was a captive here.

"Come on, Brenwar," I pleaded. "I'm ready to go. It's been three weeks already."

"Ah, but the Festival of Iron has just started. We can't leave now: you haven't even seen the best part yet," he replied, marching down a crowded street.

The opening parade had begun a week ago, and it hadn't finished yet. The dwarves only celebrated the Festival of Iron once in a decade, and they put a lot of effort into it. I stopped to watch as a regiment of dwarves marched by in full plate armor, with only their beards and weapons hanging out. They were in perfect cadence, every booted foot in step, not one out of a thousand dwarves out of line.

"How many soldiers are there, anyway?" I

asked, looking over Brenwar's head. I was the tallest person in the entire city, at the moment, anyway.

"Oh, I can't tell you that, but I might entertain a guess."

I'd been asking questions every day for weeks. It helped pass the time. A certain question in particular always came to mind: "When are we leaving?" Still, I had to respect my host.

"One Hundred Thousand?" I said.

"No."

"Fifty Thousand?"

"No."

"Can you give me a hint?"

A tiny dwarven boy was standing on the shoulders of his father, smiling at me and holding nine fingers up.

"Ninety..." I said.

The dwarven boy, whose beard had not started yet, showed six fingers.

"—Six thousand?"

Brenwar turned. I could see the surprise in his stony face. His eyes flitted from me to the boy and back to me when he said, "Humph... close enough." He eyed the boy again, stroking his beard, and said, "Ye should mind your own business."

I put my arm over Brenwar and walked him away, saying, "Ah. It's no wonder you all look so grumpy all the time. You don't encourage fun when you're young."

"Fun is for the foolish. A dwarf's work is never done. We don't run around looking for things to smile about all the time."

"You would if you could smile like me," I grinned.

He shook his head, saying, "That smile would be much prettier accompanied by a nice long beard."

I rubbed my clean-shaven face. I was the only beardless man in the Morgdon, aside from the women and children. Of course, many of the women did have beards, and I never got used to that. It just didn't seem natural, a fuzzy-faced woman, but they could all cook a delicious feast. I'd give them that.

"Brenwar, honestly, when can we leave?"

I was restless. Now that I had a white spot on my dragon hand, I wanted to save the Dragons more than ever. I felt like a piece of me was back, like my honor had returned. I wasn't motivated before, but now I was more motivated than ever. And I couldn't help but wonder: *What do the white scales mean?*

"Soon, Dragon. Come now," he said, reaching over and grabbing a tankard of ale from the booth of a dwarven Ale Master. He quaffed it down in one gulp and belched like a man-sized bullfrog. He patted his belly and grabbed another round and thrust it in my face. "Drink and be merry. Be merry and drink."

"I'm fine, thanks. Now, Brenwar, let's go," I groaned. "You know I have Dragons to fetch."

"Wait until the song's over," he said with a wink.

"What song?" I said. "There's no one singing."

That's when I saw a smile from behind his beard as he raised his booming voice to the clouds and sang:

"HOOOOOOOOOOOOOOOOOOOOOO…"

Instantly, thousands of dwarves joined in.

"Home of the dwarves! Morgdon! Home of the dwarves! Morgdon!

We make the finest steel and ale. Morgdon! In battle, we never fail! Morgdon!

Home of the dwarves! Morgdon! Home of the dwarves! Morgdon…"

The singing went on and on, and I'd be lying if I said I didn't enjoy it. As much as I didn't want to sing, I couldn't help but do just that. The robust dwarves put everything they had into the moment. They jumped, swung, tapped, drank and sang all at the same time. I'd never seen so many happy dwarves before, and it made me happy, too. There was no better army in all Nalzambor than an army of dwarves. They'd fight until their hearts were black and blue.

"Home of the dwarves! Morgdon! Home of the dwarves! Morgdon!

We make the toughest armor and ale. Morgdon! In battle, we never turn tail! Morgdon!

Home of the dwarves! Morgdon! Home of the dwarves! Morgdon…"

When it ended, I was fulfilled. The dwarves were ready for anything. I was ready for anything.

Brenwar slapped me on the back and said, "What did you think of that?"

"I liked it!"

I decided I should make the most of it. You just couldn't let every day of your life be filled with worry. "Trust in the greater good instead," my Father would say. So I did. After all, Morgdon was a fantastic city with the boldest architecture I ever saw. A suspension bridge crossed from one side of Morgdon to another. The buildings and towers were all square-cut stone, but not just any stone: many stones of many colors, not bright, but not all dull, either. Where you didn't see stone, you saw metal. Burnished, hammered, polished or riveted, it adorned their bodies, faces, buildings and all places.

"Look at this, Dragon! Ho! You are in for a treat!" Brenwar pointed.

The parade was still going strong. The regiment of dwarves had marched on, but I could still hear their heavy boots pounding the ground like a steady heartbeat. I followed Brenwar's arm that pointed upward. A group of dwarven men were sitting in the sky.

"How are they doing that?"

They each sat in a tiny seat at the top of a pole that was ten stories tall, four of them in all. Beneath them, big dwarves with broad chests held them up on shafts of iron, eyes straight forward as they marched along. Every eye was filled with wild wonder as the dwarves stood high atop their perches and bowed.

"Are they crazy! What are they going to do?"

"Just watch, Dragon!"

A wild dragon couldn't tear my eyes away as one dwarf saluted, teetered backward, and fell.

CHAPTER 2

THE CROWD GASPED AS ONE dwarf fell, followed by another and another until the fourth one fell. My heart jumped in my chest as they plummeted to the ground amid the frightened streams. Certainly, there was a net, a magic spell or something to save them from breaking their necks? As much as I wanted to be, even I wasn't fast enough or close enough to catch any of them.

"Brenwar, they're going to—"

The first dwarf was caught by two others.

The second was caught by two more, and so on, and so on. The crowd erupted in cheers as the falling dwarves bowed and raced back up the poles to the delight of the crowd.

Brenwar elbowed me in the gut, saying, "Had you fooled, didn't they? Wouldn't you say?"

I didn't know what to say, actually. It didn't

seem possible for a dwarf to be caught from a ten story fall, and it even seemed less likely for one to shimmy like a spider monkey up an iron bean poll. *Maybe I should take a dwarven acrobat with me on my next adventure. Such agility would move things quicker.*

"That was incredible, Brenwar! I'd like to meet—"

"Hah!" He waggled his finger at me. "I know what you're thinking about them dwarves. They might be acrobatic, but they can't fight worth a hoot. Humph."

"Is that so?" I said, surprised. "I thought all dwarves could fight."

"They can," Brenwar grabbed a loaf of bread stuffed with pepperoni and took a bite, "better than men, orcs and elves that is. But they're not dwarven soldiers. Dwarven acrobats is all, the best acrobats in all of Nalzambor!"

"Certainly."

The next few hours, I allowed myself to unwind and take in more of the city of Morgdon and all its rugged exteriors. They could hammer iron so thin that you could see right through it. An entire building was windowed with it. "No rock or arrow could shatter that iron glass," Brenwar boasted. There were so many objects and artifices of iron that it was just incredible, but as the sun began to set and the fervor of the festival renewed its rise, I realized it was time to go.

"Brenwar, I think I'm going to head back to your place and take a break," I said, walking away.

"What? But the festival has just begun!" he said, not looking at me but chewing his pepperoni loaf and watching the acrobats instead. "Just stay and watch a few hours more."

I could see he was enjoying himself, but frankly, I'd had my fill. And the white spot inside my dragon palm looked a tad smaller. I had to save more Dragons; I just had to.

"I'll see you later, Brenwar," I said, waving.

"Wait a moment, Dragon!" he said, stopping me in my tracks. "Remember, you cannot leave Morgdon without me, and every dwarf in the city knows that. So you go rest and stay put. I've a few ceremonies to attend to."

I nodded.

He eyed me.

"What?" I said. I could see he wanted confirmation from me, a promise that I would not leave, but I wasn't going to give him that. Never make a promise you can't keep. Just let them think it's a promise.

"Give me your word, Dragon."

I shook my head, saying, "Why bother? I can't leave anyway. A thousand eyes are on me. My Brenwar, I'm as much a prisoner as a guest."

"Prisoner?" he stroked his beard. "That's not polite, and you know it!" He combed his fingers through his beard and muttered under his breath. "Better be no pixies in there." Then he looked at me. "As for you, a prisoner? Pah! I'm looking out for you. That's all. Don't be hasty, Dragon."

"Every day we stay, the graver the danger gets for the dragons."

"You can't save them all, try as you might."

I glared at him.

"What if it were dwarves we were going to rescue? Would you wait then?"

"Ho! A dwarf needing rescued!" Brenwar laughed. "I've never seen such a thing. Nobody poaches dwarves. Not if they know what's good for them."

"Well, nobody poaches orcs, either!" I said, storming away.

"What!" Brenwar yelled at me. "You take that back, Dragon!"

I kept going.

He kept yelling.

"And don't you dare try to leave without me!"

Brenwar's home was small and quiet. His children were grown, and his wife was working at the festival. Such a fine cook she was, one of the finest I'd ever known. Still, it was good to be alone with my thoughts. If I wanted to pout, I'd pout alone.

I pulled up a stool on the balcony overlooking the vast and colorful city. It seemed like every torch and pyre was alive with yellow, green, red, orange and even pink fires. The air smelled of roasted everything good, too, and I hungered.

"I can't wait any longer," I mumbled. I wanted to pass over the great wall that held Morgdon, dash over the plains below, and save the dragons. Holding my dragon hand before me, I studied it with intent. Was I getting close? Could I remove the evil curse on my own? But part of me wondered what would happen without my dragon arm. Making two fists, I punched one into the other. I could feel that extra power within me. Something great. It was part of me—the strongest part—and I didn't want to do without it.

Rubbing the white scales of my hand, I said to myself, "I wonder if the white are as strong as the black?" Standing up, I leaned over the balcony and looked as far out as I could see. There were dragons out there who needed me. And I needed them as well. But how could I get out of Morgdon without anyone finding out?

As the bats darted in and out of the night sky snatching the fireflies in their mouths, I snapped my fingers.

"That's a great idea, Dragon! A great one!"

I dashed inside Brenwar's place, found my pack and his, and tossed them both on my bed along with my longsword Fang and my bow Akron. I wouldn't be going anywhere without them. I counted the arrows in my quiver. I had hunting arrows, Moorite tipped arrows, and magic arrows for extraneous circumstances, plus one that I wasn't certain at all what it would do, but supposedly it would do what I told it to do. "Can't wait to use you," I said, taking it out and stroking its bright red feathers before sticking it back in. "Now what?"

I dug into Brenwar's pack. He'd kill me if he knew I was doing that, especially because he liked to keep things tidy, and I was not tidy, not by a dwarf's standards, not even close. I found a jeweled case trimmed in gold with a dragon-faced hasp. It was just what I was looking for. Opening it, I found two dozen vials filled with colorful liquids. Potions. And not just any potions, magic potions. I plucked three of them out. One of them was light blue, a healer. If I was leaving without Brenwar, I'd need to be more careful. The second, dark blue, a concealer. The third I shook in front of my face. The yellow colors swirled with white. "I hope this is it," I said as I closed the lid and put the jeweled case back in his pack as neatly as I could.

"I'd take the whole thing with me if I could," I said to myself.

It was heavy though, like a hundred stones. I could barely carry it, but Brenwar had little trouble at all with his pack. It was my father's design, no doubt about that, filled with all kinds of magic from my father's trove. I was blessed, that much was certain, that my father allowed Brenwar to take the pack and be its guardian.

I slipped into my chest plate armor, strapped my sword on my waist, then snapped my bow in place. Slinging my pack over my shoulder, I was ready to go now. I pulled the cork out of the yellow vial, stepped out onto the balcony, and started to drink.

"Oh wait," I said.

I left Brenwar a note.

Dear Brenwar,

The dragons can't wait, and I can't either.

Forgive me,

Nath Dragon

He would be furious, but I couldn't wait a moment longer. I yearned for freedom, not just mine, but for the dragons. They needed me. I put the vial to my lips and took the first sip. It tasted like berries and honey.

"Mmmmm' I said, smacking my lips.

A moment later, I pitched forward and fell to my knees as my mind turned to mud.

CHAPTER
3

EVERYTHING TURNED BLACK. SOMETHING was wrong. Terribly wrong. I couldn't see a thing, but my ears were just fine. I could hear everything in the street below but much louder this time.

What do I do! What have I done! That potion has me undone!

My plan was simple: take the potion of polymorph and turn myself into something else. I stretched out and fluttered on the floor. This shouldn't have been so hard; I'd done it before. But, I'd never turned myself into a bat.

"Eek!" I screamed, but it came out a high pitched shriek.

Bats are blind, you idiot!

What was I thinking? Oh, now I remember. I was going to blend in with the bats and fly away.

None of the keen eyed dwarfs would pay attention to such a thing.

Think! Take a breath, Dragon. You can figure this out.

I flapped my wings. Nothing. I rose on my tiny clawed feet and flapped once more. I lifted from the ground. *Yes!* I banged into a wall and plummeted back to the floor. *Ow!*

At least, I thought it was a wall; I couldn't see it. Head aching, I made my next attempt.

Up, Dragon!

Whop!

I hit something else and dove nose first into the floor. *Think, Dragon. Think!*

Morphing into a new body took some getting used to, and it didn't help that I was blind to boot, and—fair enough—I was stupid, too. I should have just turned into a bird. I rubbed my nose with the tiny fingers at the end of my wing and sniffed the air. Not only could I hear everything, I could smell everything as well. Pretty amazing. What I lacked in sight, I made up with everything else.

What else could bats do that I didn't know about? I had to think on that. Then I remembered they had a sonic power that helped them out.

"Eek!"

That wasn't it. I tried something else. A whisper of sorts. Soon after I let it out, an echo came back. *Ah! I get it now!*

I lifted my head up and sounded out towards the smells and sounds below. In my mind, I saw the shape of the balcony now. Gathering myself, I fluttered to the ledge. *Made it!* Then I took a deep breath. Well, as big a breath as I could, that is. I certainly felt like I was in a very small body. I sent out a signal. The bats and bugs were still there, but the rest of my path from Morgdon was all clear. *Here we go... Bat Dragon!*

I slipped from the ledge, spread my wings, and *whoosh*—I was flying! Everything in my body was tingling, making me all the more eager to become a dragon one day. Then a thought struck me. Not all dragons can fly. What if I was one of those? No, I must perish such thoughts; it shouldn't matter either way. Right now, I needed to enjoy that I was free!

I let out a signal. Moths and fireflies fluttered in the air, and a strange hunger came over me. I signaled again, and like a beacon, I knew where the firefly was. I zoomed in and snatched it in my mouth. That was fast! I liked that. *Yech!* It left an odd taste in my mouth, *but* I crunched it up anyway.

Time to move on, Dragon! The sooner you go the better. No telling when the potion's magic would wear off, and I didn't want to be in the air when that happened, either. I let out a new signal. The mountain was behind, but the open plains of

Nalzambor were below. That's where I went, where the goat herders go.

Flap! Flap! Flap!

Something soared past me. What was that? I ducked and dove before I got a good look around. The other bats were attacking me. One after the other they came, nipping and clawing at me. What were they attacking me for? All I ate was one lousy firefly. It wasn't like there weren't plenty of them left out there, you know. But in full assault they came. I was in trouble now.

I shrieked. It didn't help. I dodged.

They struck.

I dove.

They bit. They were going to drive me from the sky.

I wanted to say something, but I don't think bats talked; they shrieked. *What would happen if they got me on the ground?* I was certain they'd tear me to shreds.

Ouch!

One of them got a piece of my leathery wing, sending me spiraling downward. I wanted to swing my sword, but it was part of me now, as well as all those other things. I regained my balance and dove into the alley of the city. Perhaps I could shake them from my trail; I understood things about the city that they did not. Maybe that would help. I flapped hard and fast, weaving into alleys and underneath bridges, drawing some cries from the crowds. I don't think the dwarves had ever seen bats chasing bats before. This might not be such a good idea, after all.

Clack. Clack. Clack.

Too late. Stones were clattering off the walls. The children were throwing stones now. Accurate ones, too. I flew under one and over another, one stone clipping the wing on a pursuer. It bought me time. Up I went. Down I came to find the bats in front of me. I was chasing them now. I sent out a signal. The one in the back, bigger than the rest, was driving the colony of bats. I knew what I had to do. I had to stop him, else they'd wear me down. I let out an awful screech. A challenge was my intent. Up, up, up! The big bat came after me.

Bat or man, I knew how to fight, and I'd fight anything anywhere. I wasn't sure how bat fights went, but I think the leader got the message. I circled him, and he circled me, then in rush he came right at me.

Whop!

We clocked heads. Blind, I saw stars, and I realized his head was much bigger and harder than mine. *I swear; with one gulp, he could eat me. What kind of bat did I turn myself into, anyway?* The more I flapped, the more my wings began to tire. Flying all the time could be very exhausting.

I sucked it up, flying straight upward as he

barreled straight downward. At the last second, I dodged, and the others were upon me, clipping and biting at me. It seemed either I fought one of them head on, or I fought them all at once. The leader and I darted up and down in a wide circle. This was it: him and me, head to head for all the glory of the nighttime bug eating. I let out my final signal. He let out his. He charged. I charged and let out my 'Dragon! Dragon!' screech. There was no need to close my eyes, but I think I did.

CHAPTER 4

I FELT SOMETHING BURNING IN MY stomach and projecting from my mouth. The big bat screeched in the sky. I let out a sonic signal. The big bat was engulfed in flames and plummeting toward the ground. I could smell it burning—its hair, its wings—as I dove after it. *Where did that flame come from? Did it come from me*?

My mouth was hot, and I could taste the bitterness of sulfur on my tongue. Below me, the burning bat crashed into a rooftop. *Yes! What kind of bat am I, anyway*? I'd never seen a fire-breathing bat before. I swooped up into the sky where the other bats waited and let out a screech of triumph. I felt another streak of flames shoot from my mouth into the sky. I sent out another sonic signal, and all the bats were gone. I'd won.

I could hear shouts and cries from bellow and

had visions of stubby fingers pointing in the sky. I flapped my way past the walls of Morgdon over and beyond where the green grass grows and flew through the night, exhausted, until I could fly no more.

I awoke to find myself in a very cramped cave with the new day's light creeping in.

"Sunken Sulfur! Where am I? Where are my arms and legs?"

I could see again, but I couldn't move a thing. It was as if I'd been nailed inside a coffin. I struggled and strained, wiggling my shoulder loose, then my arm and leg.

"Ah… I'm whole again," I said, crawling out of the cramped cave. "Whoa!" I tumbled down a rocky hillside and went crashing into the hard ground below. "Stupid!" *What was I thinking, turning into a bat? I almost got myself killed. And being blind wasn't any fun at all.* Next time I changed, it would be into something else, but I had to admit: all the flying was incredible.

I dusted myself off, and to my relief, everything was intact: my sword, my bow, and even my pack. You have to like magic like that, which transforms not only you, but everything you carry as well. "Thank goodness."

Above me, the sun was rising, and Morgdon was nowhere in sight. The last thing I remembered was flying as far and fast as I could, putting the Festival of Iron far behind. Guilt crept into me, however, about leaving Brenwar behind. I knew he'd be mad, but I also knew that he didn't understand. He was a dwarf; I was part dragon, part man. He'd just have to understand.

I coughed. The inside of my stomach churned like a pot of boiling lava, and the taste of sulfur was still inside my mouth.

Smacking my lips, I said, "That tastes horrible." I stuck a finger in my mouth, feeling around, certain I'd find a piece of charred wood inside there. What happened, anyway? Could bats breathe fire? Impossible.

I coughed again. No smoke. No fire. Doing my best impression of a dragon, I forced out a roar of air. Nothing came out.

"Hmmm... perhaps it was a side of effect of the potion," I said to myself. That happens, you know. I shrugged it off. It was time to go, but where to? I stretched my arms and limbs and raked my fingers through my hair.

"Freedom!" I yelled, stirring the birds in the trees. "Ha-Ha-Ha-Ha!"

I ran! Long legs cutting through the woodland like a wild stag's, I ran hard and long, with nowhere in mind to go. I was free. Not that I'd been a slave, but without Brenwar tagging along, I was liberated. Too often, he'd slow me down and nag.

"Quit looking at your arm."

"Focus, Dragon. Focus."

"Slow down."

"I need ale."

"Did I ever tell you about the time I killed an ettin?"

It wasn't all that bad, most of the time, but there was nothing like being alone without anyone to answer to. I could do what I wanted now, and I was going to. This time, I was going to rescue many dragons on my own. *I think that might better help my cause.*

I ran several leagues before I came to a stop beneath a shady tree and took a seat. Wind in my hair, civilization long from sight, I had all the peace and quiet I ever wanted.

"Ah, now this is the life!"

Finger on the white scaled spot in the middle of my dragon hand, I found relief.

"I guess it's alright to kill bats, then." And why wouldn't it be? After all, that bat was picking on me. I tapped my fist on my chest as another fit of coughing began, but the taste of sulfur in my mouth was gone. "Finally! That's much better." I took a pull from the canteen in my pack.

It was midday now, and I had a lot on my mind. Where was I going to go to find the dragons? And

I didn't want to find just one. I wanted to find several at a time. I knew they were out there and that the most likely spot was one of the Clerics of Barnabus temples that were scattered and hidden throughout the world.

"Not a good idea," I said, rubbing my scales on my dragon arm. Such a fascinating thing, it was. I tried to imagine what it would look like in white. "If I was a careless dragon, where would I go? Hmmmm." I also wanted to get as much distance between me and Morgdon as possible, and I had to think about that as well. *If Brenwar came after me, where would he think I'd go?* Nalzambor is a very large place with each major city several hundred leagues from the other.

The Free City of Narnum was the closest and filled with the most trouble, the kind I like, that is. Pretty faces from all the other places gather there in celebration.

The Home of the Elves, Elomehorrahahn, or Elome for short, is a fantastic place hidden in the mist and trees. Their surrounding forests are well guarded as they like their privacy, and as far as I knew, they didn't meddle with dragons. They were jealous is what I always figured.

Thraag, or Thraagramoor, the home of the orcs, is simply too smelly to go near. I'd had my fill for a while in Orcen Hold.

That left Morgdon, that I had to avoid, and Quintuklen, where I hadn't been for a while. The humans lived there, and I'd had some friends there. Perhaps it was time I checked with some. I missed their colorful ways and wonderful things. The humans had the most zeal for life compared to all the others, simply put: because they didn't live so long. They gave "living life to the fullest" new meaning, and I could relate to them better than the rest. Especially now, when I had a sense of urgency within me.

But, Quintuklen was a long way off, and I could probably rescue a dozen dragons by the time I got there. But, there were many men and women in that city that knew an awful lot about dragons. Humans had poachers as well. Wizards, clerics, sages—many of them with questionable character—wanted the dragons, our magic and the secrets that we held.

I could hear Brenwar's voice in my head as if he was here saying, "There's nothing but troubles and temptation for you in the cities." I sighed. I was focused. I could handle those distractions now if need be.

And of course, there were still all the small cities, towns and villages spread out and in between. I would just head that way first.

"Perhaps I should buy a horse."

I had a long, long way to go.

By nightfall, I'd made it to a small town called Quinley, a thriving farming community. The buildings were well constructed, the people amiable but wary. I respected their hard-working kind, but I was certain they didn't care for a stranger like me. I fit in like a shiny button on a potato sack shirt. Not that they were dirty, but grubby from all their hard work. I almost opted to remain outside to avoid the stares, but the steady rain convinced me otherwise, so I entered. My coins were as good as any, and I was certain they wouldn't mind my business, so inside the nearest establishment I went.

My stomach growled as the scent of hot food aroused my senses. I could taste the roasted lamb and baked rolls in my mouth already. One thing about the well-fed people in the countryside: nobody made better buttered bread—and the vegetables were always fresh and delicious. Patting my tummy, I smiled as I walked in, keeping my dragon arm concealed under my cloak.

"Can I help you, er, Sir?" the innkeeper asked. He was tall and lean with a nice head of brown hair, for a man. He wore overalls underneath his apron and had a white scar on his clean-shaven chin. It was probably from some sort of farming accident as a child. He seemed alright, but his eyes were busy.

"I need food and a room for the night," I said.

"Eh," he started, wiping his greasy fingers on his apron, "we don't have any more rooms."

He was lying. There was no one else on the floor except me, him and a table where a young couple sat. A pair of passersby like me, judging by their traveling cloaks and boots. They eyed me. I eyed them back until they turned away. I looked the innkeeper square in the eyes.

"Are you sure you don't have any rooms? I'd hate to think I came all this way, to the wonderful town of Quinley, home of the finest carrots and heifers, only to find they don't have any rooms. Perish the thought!"

The innkeeper showed me a toothy smile as he leaned back and I leaned forward.

"Er... it's true."

The innkeeper jumped as I rapped my knuckles on the bar.

"Well that's just horrible!" I said. And it really was, for him, because I was starting to get mad. I didn't like it when people lied, and it was even worse when they did it without batting an eye. Something strange, very strange was going on in Quinley. But, that wasn't any of my business. Getting some hot food and a dry room was. I continued.

"And I suppose you are out of *food,* too?"

The innkeeper nodded his head.

A comely older woman emerged from the kitchen with two plates full of hot food. She stumbled as she saw me, eyes blinking, as she plopped the meals onto the couple's table. The woman turned towards me, pushed her hair back, straightened her shoulders, and smiled before casually making her way back to the kitchen. I smiled back and waved. Then I turned my attention back to the innkeeper.

"I suppose that was your last meal... eh, Innkeeper?"

Palms up, he shrugged, smiled and said, "Y-Yes."

LIAR!

Now, I was hungry. Really, really hungry. And tired. I wanted food, and a room, and they were going to give it to me. *Liar, Liar, Britches on fire!* And all those years, I'd thought the country folk were nice.

"What are you eating over here?" I said, walking over to the other travelers. "Smells good!" Something was wrong here. Why would they serve this ordinary man and woman, but not me? Sure, I had beautiful gold eyes and a wonderful mane of auburn hair, on the frame of an extraordinary man, but that's no reason to exempt me. Is it?

"Go away," the man said, hand falling to a small dagger at his side. "Just passing through, and we don't want any trouble."

"I don't want any trouble either, my friends. But I really don't want to sleep in the rain." I turned back to the Innkeeper. "Or on an empty stomach!"

A silence fell over the room. I could sense the

Innkeeper didn't want any trouble, but I was certain he'd seen stranger men than me before. There were many other races that had come into this place. I could tell by all the unique objects that decorated the walls: elven shoes, a dwarven shovel and even the two-pronged forks of the orcs.

The waitress returned, a swagger in her hips, a smile on her lips, and a bowl of soup with a biscuit in her hands.

"Jane, no," the innkeeper warned, reaching for her.

Dipping her shoulder and shuffling over to me, she nodded and said, "Take this quick, and go."

I took the bowl from her and said, "Thank you, but why?"

She stared up at me and said nothing as she licked her lips.

That happens sometimes.

"Jane is it?" I said. "That's a pretty blouse you're wearing, and your eyes and ears, so pretty. Are you part-elven?"

She blushed.

"No, none at all."

"Jane! Get back in the kitchen! You're causing trou—"

Two large men pushed through the door, each soaked from head to toe. One cursed the rain, the other shouted out loud.

"Ale! Food! Now, Innkeeper. It's a lousy night,

so it better be good. And none of that watered-down brew you have, either."

"You should have gone," Jane whispered. "It's not safe here." She scurried back to the kitchen.

Behind me, the couple were taut as bowstrings, heads down, chewing quietly.

I had the feeling they weren't expecting these men's company.

"As you wish, Enforcers," The innkeeper said, fixing two tankards. "Right away!"

The men tossed their cloaks on a rack in the corner. Thick-shouldered and heavy, each wore steel on his hip: sword and dagger. Strong chinned, beady eyed and rugged, they had the look of Enforcers. It seemed the friendly farm city of Quinley was under control of an unfriendly element. They were the kind that riled me.

Sluuuu-urp!

"Mmmm... that's good soup," I said. "You should try some, fellas."

Both men perked up, big hands falling to their swords. I don't think they were accustomed to anyone else's voice in the room, especially one as deep and rich as mine. They looked at each other and then the innkeeper, and one said, "I told you not to welcome any strangers."

The innkeeper set the tankards down and said, "I d-didn't, Sir. I told him we had no food and no rooms, but he's persistent."

One enforcer slid back out the door. The taller one's eyes drifted to my sword Fang that hung from the scabbard. He swallowed first before he said, "This inn is closed, Traveler. Set your soup down and be gone." He nodded at the door.

"But it's raining," I said, "And I'm really tired and hungry. So, I don't think I'll be leaving right away. But, maybe tomorrow."

"Don't be a fool, Traveler. You don't know who you're tangling with."

I wanted to laugh, but I slurped another spoonful instead. The big man's eyes started to twitch. I don't think he was accustomed to anyone standing up to him. *I should be worried about who I'm tangling with? He's the one who should be worried.*

"Tell you what," I said, digging my spoon deeper into my bowl. "How about you leave, ugly face and all, and come back tomorrow when I'm well rested and gone?"

"What!"

The innkeeper ducked behind the counter. The couple behind me got up from their table, heads down, and darted up the stairs.

"I'm sorry," I said much louder this time, "I didn't realize you had trouble hearing. I SAID—"

A half-dozen well-armed men burst through the entrance—and one of them was bigger than two put together.

CHAPTER 5

NSIDE THE PILLARS OF AN old temple ruin, Finnius the Cleric of Barnabus was brewing something. Trouble.

"In order to catch a dragon, you have to have a dragon," he muttered, adding some ingredients to a mystic pot of stew. "Shaved scales and ogre nails. Blood from a vorpal snail." He sniffed the bubbling cauldron. "Yech. I never really did like this part." He covered his nose with the sleeve of his robes, saying, "Anything for High Priestess Selene." On he went, one more defiling component after another as the smell and activity of the cauldron became stronger and stronger.

"One more thing is all," he said, wiping the sweat from his head, then wringing his hands. He produced a tiny vial of blood Selene had given him. She told him it was the key ingredient of the spell.

He dumped it in, and the entire cauldron lurched, smoked, sparked with gold fire, then bubbled and dimmed.

"Acolytes, bring me the prisoner." He smiled. "It's ready."

Yes, catching the bait, the yellow streak dragon, was one step. Luring Nath Dragon was the next, and it would be awfully hard to lure someone with bait when you didn't know where he was. The last he had heard, Nath Dragon had been in the Shale Hills. Many of the clerics had reported this, but that was weeks ago, and Nath Dragon hadn't been heard from since.

"Must find him. Must find him soon," he said.

The High Priestess was very clear about that. She wanted results. She had expectations, or she'd have his head. The fact that she'd taken a shine to him was odd, but he knew he had skills that others did not. He figured at some point she must have noticed.

"Ah, here you come," he said, taking a seat on a stone bench.

Two acolytes approached, robed from head to toe in dark purple with silver trim. Their heads were bald, and the tattoos on them were very little. They were expendable at this point. They each carried what looked to be a large covered bird cage with them. Bowing, they set it down.

Finnius crossed his legs and draped his locked fingers over his knee.

"Hmmmm."

The truth was: he wasn't so certain if this would work or not, but he didn't have any other ideas, either. Typically, when Nath Dragon entered one of the larger cities, he knew about it immediately. The Clerics of Barnabus were thick in those places, and the man was about as discreet in his activities as a weasel in a hen house. But of late, Nath Dragon had been laying low, and that complicated things. Selene's expectations must be met. He wasn't about to disappoint *her*.

He lifted the cloth cover from the first cage. A man, standing about one foot tall, stood inside, tiny arms crossed over his little chest. He had two wings. Like a humming bird's, they buzzed on and off behind him. He was a pixlyn: rare, and almost impossible to catch unless you had honey from the trees where the stump giants sat.

"The time has come to earn your freedom, little pixlyn."

It turned away.

"Oh, come now. It won't be so bad," Finnius said, digging a large spoon into the bubbling cauldron. "Besides, failure to carry out my order will result in certain death."

The pixlyn shrugged. He was a handsome and obstinate little thing whose eyes glowed with a faint blue fire.

Finnius snorted as he approached, holding the spoon of bubbling goo up to the bars.

The pixlyn held his nose.

"Oh, I suggest you reconsider," Finnius said, nodding to the other acolyte. "Especially since it's not you I'm threatening.

The man removed the cloth from the other cage.

"It's her."

The pixlyn man let out a tiny cry of alarm. A beautiful pixlyn woman with radiant pink eyes and bee's wings shivered inside her cage. The pixlyn man's hummingbird wings made an angry buzz as he zipped back and forth in his cage, slamming into one barred side and then the other.

Finnius laughed. He loved seeing good creatures suffer, and it was especially salivating when it was the suffering of one loved one for another.

"Settle down now, Pixlyn. All you have to do is seek, find and report. Of course, what you'll be searching for could be anywhere in all of Nalzambor. Now, take a sip, a big one that will fill your little gut, and on your way you shall go."

The tiny little woman rose up in her cage, her squeaky little voice objecting in a language only the pixie-kind could speak. Both their tiny little hands grabbed the bars as they faced each other. Tears went down the little woman's cheeks.

"How adorable," Finnius said. "Now drink!" He banged the cage with his hand. "Or I'll kill you both right now!"

Dejected, the little pixlyn man grabbed the spoon, gulped it down and wiped his mouth.

"Good... Good-Good-Good. That will make you strong and help you find Nath Dragon's trail." He opened the bird cage door. "Go now, go! The longer it takes, the less likely she lives."

The pixlyn grabbed her tiny hands on the bars, kissed them each and with the speed of an arrow, disappeared.

As the tiny woman sobbed in her prison, Finnius tossed one of his men an empty vial and said, "Get me those tears."

CHAPTER 6

NOW THERE WERE SIX OF them and one of me. They had leather armor and swords, and even helmets on, too. Not the kind of odds I expected in a small town like this. And to think, all I wanted was a room for the night and some food.

"Sorry fellas, but I think I just finished the last bit of food," I said, setting the bowl on the table. I patted my belly and burped. "Pretty tasty though, worth the wait until tomorrow. Say, any of you ugly men happen to have a toothpick on you?"

"Shut your mouth," the one who'd hung back in the room said. He came closer, the rest of the enforcers at his sides and spreading out except one, the big one, abnormally large, who looked like he had part giant in him. He was almost eight feet tall, and his big and meaty arms were crossed over his barrel chest as he blocked the exit.

I backed up until I bumped into the table. What was I going to do now? I couldn't fight them all, or could I? They came closer, wary, weathered and scarred, one just as mean looking as the other. A well-trained bunch of goons, mercenary and ex-soldiers types, men for hire judging by the steel jangling on their hips. They were the kind of men who wouldn't hesitate to hurt or kill.

I put my hands out in front of me.

"Perhaps, I should be going. I don't think a little bit of rain ever hurt anyone, eh?"

When facing a conflict of superior enemies, play nice before the first dagger strikes.

"Oh, ho-ho," the leader said, swinging his sword up on his shoulder. "So you want to play nice now, do you, Smart Fella? What's the matter? Are we too ugly for you?"

"As a matter of fact, yes, but that's not the reason I'm willing to leave."

The enforcers snickered as they drew their daggers.

"It's nothing personal," I said, "I mean, yes you are ugly, not like an orc, well except you," I pointed at one with the turned-up nose, "and you."

"Be silent, you fool! You've crossed the line, Big Mouth. And to think, all you had to do was walk out when I said, but now you'll have to pay. Possibly with your life, you golden eyed-freak!"

A heavy thumping pounded inside my chest.

They meant business. I slid between the table and the wall. They came closer. I didn't need this kind of trouble.

"Tell you what, uh, what do you call yourselves?"

"Enforcers, Fool!"

"So it is, Enforcers Fool. Very catchy. Now here is what I offer. Leave me be, and I'll see to it that you can walk out of here, not crawl… or die."

They snickered.

"You've got a death wish, do you! So be it! Enforcers, take him!"

I stuck out my dragon arm.

They hesitated, eyes going back and forth between each other.

"What's the matter? Never seen a dragon's arm on a man before?"

Even the big one gawped and scratched his balding head.

I had them now. I had them right where I wanted them. I shoved the table aside, stepped forward, and towered over them, except the one in the back of course.

"Men! What are you waiting for? We've taken down plenty of stranger things before, but never one with a mouth so big. And do I have to remind you who your lord is? The Jackal will not be pleased if you fail him in this. Now, don't make me tell you again, Enforcers. Attack!"

They surged forward, striking high and low.

I leapt into the rafters. This isn't what I wanted. Not at all. These men were killers, and they wanted me dead. I couldn't stay up here forever. There was only one rafter and nowhere to go.

"Brock! Get over there and jerk that bird out of those rafters!"

The over-sized man made it across the room in three strides, reaching up my way. His big fingers reached at my feet as I kicked them away.

"Go away, Brock!"

He was big and ugly, but not stupid. He laughed.

"Get him, Brock!"

"Snap his neck like a chicken's!"

"I've got dibs on his pretty hair!"

I kicked Brock in the nose, drawing a painful howl. That last comment lit a fire in me. My problem was they could kill and seemed perfectly willing to, but I could not. Problem.

Brock threw his shoulder into the post. The entire building shook.

The innkeeper was screaming, "Stop it! Stop it!"

The leader shoved him to the ground.

It seemed these enforcers had a point to make. Something weird was going on here, and The Jackal, whoever that was, was behind it all. It was time for me to move.

Brock hit the post again, cracking it and shaking the room.

I dropped on his shoulders and blinded him with my hands.

"Easy, Brock," I said. "What you can't see, you can't hit!"

"Get off of me, Rodent!"

He reached for my hands.

I slapped him on his bald head.

"That will leave a mark. Woo! My, it's hot up here."

The leader shouted out, "Brock, kneel down so we can get a lick at him!"

The fun was over. Brock dropped to a knee.

I jumped from his shoulders to one table and then another. I had to get as far away from Brock as possible. He could crush me. Jumping, ducking, diving and dodging, I got a few punches in as they chased me around the room.

"Blast it! You fools!" The leader said. "Do I have to do everything myself! Brock, guard the door! We can't let him get away."

They seemed pretty persistent about not letting me go, for some reason. Perhaps they didn't want word getting out about their indiscretions. I jumped left, right, then found myself cornered, two daggers and a sword at my throat.

"Now we've got you!"

CHAPTER 7

"**G**IVE IT UP, OR I'LL cut your throat!"

I wouldn't yield. Not to them. Not to men lacking character. And my pride wouldn't let me give in to an inferior but skilled and well-armed force, despite the numbers.

I started to speak.

The leader cut me off. "Save it! Your tongue's caused you enough trouble. Keep your peace and get ready to die, Freak!"

I was tired and no longer hungry but agitated now. I didn't like that word, Freak. I would not yield. Not to this scum. Not now. Not no-how. Especially when I was fast. Faster than them all. I could draw Fang faster than they could swing. I told myself to do it. I willed myself to do it. But I did not. I couldn't risk killing, evil men or not.

There had to be a better way; there always was, my father said.

I locked my eyes on his and summoned my magic within. Dragon magic, ancient, wonderful, accessible. I could see my reflection in the man's eyes. His hardened features slackened at the sound of my thoughts.

Lower your sword, I suggested.

"Huh," he said, shaking his head, "what did you say?"

It wasn't working. I summoned all I had within, my gold eyes glowing.

"What is that?" one said.

"A demon!" cried another.

I made my suggestion again, putting all my mental strength behind it this time.

Drop your sword!

The leader's blade clattered to the ground.

"What did you do that for?" the enforcers said.

"He's a demon, I tell you!"

Whack!

I punched the man in the jaw, dropping him like a stone.

"I'm..."

Whack!

I knocked another's helmet off.

"Not!"

Twist! Crack! Boom! Twist!

I disarmed and disabled the leader.

"A demon!"

One rushed.

I had room to move now. I dipped and struck. My dragon arm's jabs were like black lightning.

The leader struggled back to his feet.

I booted him in the ribs, lifting him from his knees. Evil men calling me a demon, such gall!

One dove on my back; another climbed on my legs.

I slung one crashing into a table and drove the other's head into the hard floor.

I was dusting my hands off and saying, "That should to it," when a large shadow fell over me. Big Brock was back.

Whop!

I crashed into the nearest wall, wondering, *how did I forget about him!*

Have you ever been hit by a log before? Me either, but I was pretty sure I knew what that felt like now. Brock was quick for a big man, not as quick as me, but as quick as an eight-foot tall man could be. And when he punched, you could feel it from one side to the other.

Bam!

My head!

Bam!

My gut!

I struggled back to my feet and raised up my fist, saying, "You want some more of this?"

Bam!

He knocked me off my feet and on my butt.

Gasping for air, I held my hands out, saying, "You don't hit very hard for a big fellow."

"What did you say?" Brock said, his voice as loud as distant thunder.

I held my nose. It was all I could do. I felt like the only thing holding my body together was my armor. "What did you say?" I mocked back. I don't know why I did that. I guess it was a character flaw that exposed itself in moments of desperation.

Brock grabbed me by my collar and with two hands, threw me across the room and into the bar. He was strong, very strong, and he hit as hard as an ogre. He came back.

I snatched Dragon Claw from Fang's hilt and stabbed him in the leg.

"Ouch."

That's all he said, "Ouch," as if I'd pricked him with a pin.

He swatted the small dagger from my hand, sending it spinning across the floor.

I was defenseless now. I was rattled. I couldn't understand why I couldn't handle this big man. I reached for the sword along my belt.

He stopped me.

"No! No! No! Demon!"

I'm not a demon!

He wrapped his arms around me as he lifted me

from the ground. My feet dangled from the floor as he squeezed the life out of me.

"How's that feel!"

I managed to say, "Great! I haven't had my back cracked in forever."

He squeezed harder. I flexed my muscles. The harder he squeezed, the more I flexed. I just hoped my bones didn't crack. The pressure was becoming unbearable.

"Give up, Demon! I've cracked bones thicker than yours before. Dwarfs, orcs, elves, I've broke them all."

Who was this man, and what was he doing in this farm village?

I snapped my head back into his chin and saw stars as he laughed.

"Any moment, you will die," he said in my ear.

He might be right. I couldn't move. I couldn't breathe. And I didn't have an ounce of magic left inside me. Maybe venturing without Brenwar was a bad idea, after all. One thing was for certain, if it wasn't for the dwarven armor I wore, I'd have been cracked like an egg already. I had to do something. Anything.

"You ate it, didn't you?" I said.

"Ate what?"

"All the food."

Wham!

He slammed me to the floor as hard as he could.

Breathless, I tried to speak, but couldn't form the words.

Brock grabbed me by the hair, jerked my head back, and wrapped his arms round my neck and throat and squeezed.

Oh no! This was bad. Very bad. Brock the giant man had me in a sleeper hold. My fingers clutched for the door, the only way of escape. I expected Brenwar to burst through at any moment, but darkness came instead.

CHAPTER

8

I WOKE UP TO THE SOUND of rattling chains. When I opened my eyes, I noticed they were mine.

"What is this! Ow!"

I clutched at my chest. My ribs were broken. The big man had gotten the best of me. It got even worse. I was inside a metal cage, very much like the ones that held dragons.

"No!" I cried.

But no one answered. Groggy and dizzy, I rubbed a strange bump on my neck. I'd been injected with something. Possibly stabbed with a tainted stick, like the savages like to use.

Two lanterns illuminated the exterior walls of what looked to be an old barn. I could hear the heavy drops of rain pounding on the ceiling above me. Large drops of water splashed on my face and back. The chains rattled as I wiped the water from my face and scooted into the corner.

"I can't believe this," I muttered to myself.

I was caged like an animal in a barn that smelled like livestock, manure and hay. I pounded my head on the bars. It hurt. But I deserved it. I'd been stupid and careless, I guess. But it wasn't as if I was looking for any trouble, either. If anything, I'd tried to avoid it. I sighed. I should have been happy that I was still alive. After all, the enforcers made it clear that they wanted me dead. And Brock, that giant of a man, could have killed me easily with his own bare hands.

Cold, tired and still hungry, I collected my thoughts. It seemed I'd have to think my way out of this. And who was my captor? Was it some sinister bunch of village folk, or the character the lead enforcer mentioned, The Jackal? How could I get into this much trouble at some silly little farm? That was when a river of ice raced down my spine.

"Fang! Akron!"

I grabbed my head and tugged at my hair. I'd lost them. And not just that, but my pack with all my supplies. No not only did my chest and neck ache, but my head did as well. And how long had I been knocked out cold? That'd only happened one time before.

I grabbed the bars and tugged.

"Hurk!"

They didn't budge. I dug my heels in.

"HURK!"

A bubble of snot formed in my nose and burst. The bars bent a little, but didn't budge from my disgusting effort. I labored for breath as I said, "Ew."

I kicked the bars. I hit the bars. I raked my dragon claws against the bars, but nothing happened. I was helpless in my cage.

And there I sat: friendless, weaponless, and helpless while the water from the roof dripped, dripped, dripped. I moved from one spot to the other, only to catch a new drip from another hole in the roof again. The barn creaked and groaned from the weight of the wind, but little stirred. No animals, no rats, no cats, no birds, which seemed strange for a place meant to keep animals. But there was something else different and unique: the smell of decay and death. On one wall were more chains, and some digging tools: spades, shovels and picks. A few work tables were spread out with hammers, anvils and saws. My eyes were good, even in the poor light, but I swore there were bloodstains.

"Not good," I said, cradling my dragon arm. What if they were going to cut it off? Perhaps they really thought I was a demon. I wasn't a demon. What an insult! I was a dragon! Well, I was part of a dragon—and any fool could see that. Perhaps it was my gold-flecked eyes that freaked them out.

"I've got to get out of here."

Grabbing the nearest bar with my dragon arm, I tugged. The iron of the cage was at least a half inch thick. The metal groaned. I could feel my black arm growing with strength. What it would not do before, it was doing now.

"Come, Dragon," I said through gritted teeth. "You can do it!"

It moved no more.

"Sultans of Sulfur!"

I collapsed against the bars.

Now my head was pounding, and my entire body was sore all over. I felt like a bruised apple from head to toe, and I could feel my face was swollen as well. On the bright side, I guess whoever it was wanted me alive. On the dark side of things, I had no idea how long it would be until I found out who that was. Cold, sore, hungry and held against my will, in pain I waited.

CHAPTER

9

"How could I be so careless!" Brenwar yelled.

A dozen well-armed dwarves stood nearby, awaiting orders.

Nath Dragon had escaped. How he escaped, Brenwar could not figure. Every dwarf in all of Morgdon knew who he was. Every dwarf in Morgdon knew that he was not supposed to leave. Every dwarf was to keep an eye on him when another wasn't. But like a ghost, he'd vanished.

Brenwar rammed his head into a stone wall.

"I can't believe it!"

He rammed it again.

"Knock some sense into yourself!" he said.

The other dwarves did the same.

Clonk. Clonk. Clonk...

"Stop it, dwarves! We don't all need our melons

damaged. We'll be needing all of our wits to track him down." He tugged at two fistfuls of beard.

Brenwar had thought he had it all under control, but he'd miscalculated. Nath had gotten into his sack and taken some potion. What they did, Brenwar didn't know, but one of them had to be the cause of all this. His investigation revealed a few other things. A small fire breathing bat was said to have been seen. Another one, as big as a large cat, was found burnt to a crisp. It had to have been Nath because no one had ever seen a fire breathing bat before. But with the Festival of Iron anything could happen. But that wasn't what haunted him most. It was what Nath's father, the grandest creature he'd ever seen, said the last time he saw him.

"I'll keep him alive, your Majesty," Brenwar had promised.

Nath's father had replied, "I'm not worried about him dying. I'm worried he'll turn evil."

Nath turning evil? It didn't seem possible, but the Dragon King's words had shaken his very core.

"Get your horses, dwarves! Get your horns as well. He's got a three-day start and could be anywhere in the world. The one that finds him gets a trunk full of gold!"

Brenwar was the last one out of the gate as they all exited with dwarven song and cheer. Brenwar took a deep breath as he watched them go, remembering another thing Nath's father had said. "If we lose him, it will begin another Dragon War."

CHAPTER 10

THE SOUND OF A BARN door opening jostled me from my sleep.

I wiped the water from my eyes and watched three figures stroll in. One was Brock, the big man, lumbering my way with the leader of the Enforcers at his side. The other man, I didn't recognize. He was lean, blond-haired and blue-eyed with my sword, Fang, hanging at his side. I would have stood up, but the cage wouldn't allow it. I sat up, and I crossed my legs as they approached.

"That's my sword," I said, glowering.

The man, light eyes intent on my arm, didn't even acknowledge me.

Rubbing his hairless chin, he said, "Peculiar, Barlow, but I don't think he's a demon. No, looks like a curse of some sort."

Barlow, an enforcer, looked at my eyes and then

said to the other man, "But his eyes glowed. All my thoughts left me, and I dropped my sword. He doesn't even have a spellbook, Jackal."

The Jackal made his way around the cage and stopped alongside the bar I'd bent.

"Too strong to be a wizard. Hmmmm. Brock, get over here and fix this. Hm, he must have done this. It's practically a new cage."

Brock lumbered over and grabbed the bar. The metal groaned as he pulled it back into position. He grunted at me as he returned to his friend.

The Jackal said, "Well, you are pretty strong. I'll give you that. Probably a good thing Renny doped you."

The leader, Renny, nodded as he folded his arms across his chest and smiled.

"Care to tell me what this is all about, Jackal?" I asked.

The Jackal wasn't a bad looking man, but there was darkness behind his beady eyes. There was something primitive about him. The way he moved was dangerous. He withdrew my sword and cut it through the air a few times.

"This," the Jackal said fingering the blade, "is amazing! Tell me where you got it. Who made it?"

Good. He wants something from me. I can use that.

"The Mountain of Doom," I said.

Fingering the dragon-head pommels on the

hilt, he said, "You jest! Am I to believe you stole it from there? No one goes into the Mountain and lives."

"That's where it's from, and that's all I know."

"So you were told," he shot back.

I shrugged. *Let him think what he wants.*

He stuffed Fang back inside the scabbard and said to his men, "You two would be dead if he had drawn this sword." Then he turned his attention back to be. "Why didn't you draw and cut them down? I would have."

"I didn't need it."

"It seems you did."

"The big fellow was fortunate, is all. Next time, I won't go so easy."

Brock and Renny laughed.

"I wish I could have been there, but perhaps I can set up another encounter."

"Why don't you set it up now?" I demanded.

Brock smacked his fist into his hand. It sounded like a clap of thunder.

"Fine by me," Brock growled.

The Jackal's eyes lit up. He liked the idea.

Good. All I have to do is get out of this cage.

"No, there will be plenty of time for that later. I need him still breathing tonight."

I don't like how he said that.

"What's the matter?" I said. "Are you afraid of Brock getting hurt?"

Brock's fist slammed into the cage.

"I'll break your neck!"

"Hah! You couldn't break a chicken leg, you oaf!"

"I'll show you!" he roared, reaching through the bars for my leg.

"BROCK, STOP IT!" Renny yelled, trying to pull the big man away.

I jammed the nail of my dragon thumb into his forearm.

Brock's howl shook the roof.

I laughed at him as Renny pulled him back.

"You're going to pay for that!" he said, shaking his fist at me.

The Jackal applauded saying, "Perfect. Just perfect... eh, sorry, I didn't get your name?"

"I didn't give it."

He waved me off, saying, "No matter. We'll think of something by tonight. Come on, men."

"What's tonight?" I said, pulling on the bars to my cage.

Renny and Brock both flashed sinister grins as they slid the barn door shut behind them.

I stomped my feet and punched the roof of the cage.

"DRAT! DRAT! DOUBLE DRAT!"

Again I was alone. To make matters worse, it seemed they had a short term plan for me: death.

I yawned. Whatever poison they stuck me with

wasn't wearing off. I spit a gummy salty substance from my mouth, leaned back, and sat down. Now was not the time to panic. It was time to think.

"Excellent, Dragon. Look what you've gotten yourself into," I said, tossing my hair over my shoulder. At least the rain had stopped. But now I was thirsty.

An hour passed.

My stomach growled. My head swam. And I was seeing black spots from time to time.

Another hour passed.

Nausea set in and cold sweat as well, and I began to shake with chills.

What did they stick me with?

I wrapped my arms around my knees and huddled in the cage. And there I lay, spinning and spinning and spinning.

CHAPTER 11

BAD PEOPLE DO BAD THINGS.

A ray of sunlight warmed my face, but it didn't stop the shivers. Time was lost to me, the minutes agony, but from the fading light coming through the cracks in the barn door, it seemed the sun was setting. I remembered the Jackal saying something about the night. Something bad was going to happen. As if it hadn't happened already.

I heard wood rubbing against metal, a horrible sound in my distorted ears. Light flooded the barn as the door was slid open. Enforcers. I couldn't see how many. The squeak of older wagon wheels felt like jamming nails in my ears.

"Hurry up and get them in there," one enforcer said. "And double check those locks. We can't have any escaping. Remember the last time. Jorkan's dead. The Jackal saw to that. And I'll not be losing my head over some busted locks!"

"You check them then!" one said.

"What? Who said that? Osclar, did you say that?"

"Yes!"

"Why you little toad eater! Get over there and check those locks, those bars, that door—or it's going to be the stockade for you! Understand!"

"Certainly, Harvey. Certainly!"

I heard the one I believed to be Harvey grunt, and I started my wait. I closed my eyes and let the shivers take over.

"What have we got here?" Harvey said. "Not feeling so spry now are you, Demon?"

"He's not a demon." I heard one say.

"What!"

"He's not a demon; that's was the Jackal said. He's cursed."

I heard Harvey chuckle.

"Oh, he's cursed alright. He probably just didn't know it till now. That Uken poison Renny stuck him with'll have him feeling and seeing all kinds of crazy things." Harvey checked the lock on the cage. "Tonight's going to really be something. You got those cages secured, Oscar!"

"Nope!" Oscar said, giggling.

Harvey grunted again.

"Shaddap and let's go; I'm hungry."

"Say, Harvey, how long do you think he'll last?"

"Shut your mouth, Oscar. The boss says no talking."

Oh, talk. Please talk.

"I don't see why not. It's not like it matters if they know what's coming or not."

"He likes the looks of surprise on their faces."

"Me too," the 3rd enforcer said.

"Let's go, chatter mouths."

My tongue clove to the roof of my mouth. *Say something, Dragon!* My quivering lips stayed sealed.

"Huh," Harvey said, "looks like this man is done already."

"He got some good licks on Big Brock, though. Never seen anyone hurt Brock before."

"Me neither."

"Shaddap you two! LET'S GO!"

Harvey's loud voice sounded like an explosion in my ears. I couldn't even open my eyes to see as I heard them walk out and slide the barn door closed.

Idiot. All I had learned was things were not only as bad as before but worse.

I shivered and shivered. I needed the Uken poison to wear off. *Fight it, Dragon! Fight!* The darkness came, leaving me alone in the barn with two torches and two new cages. I managed to open my eyes to see. Two forms huddled, one in each cage. Perhaps they could tell me something. I opened my mouth, but no words came.

"Father?"

It was the voice of a young man speaking to the other.

"Sssssh, be silent, Son. Else they'll whip us."

Silence came. A little rustling around followed.

"Are they going to kill us, Father?" the young man asked.

"No, now be silent!" the father said, forcefully, but quiet.

I heard the fear in both their voices. Innocent men. I could tell.

"Why did they pick us, Father?"

The father sighed, shaking his head as he said, "I don't know; they just did."

"But we were good farmers, Father. Good miners, too. I didn't steal any of the golden ore; I swear," the young man sobbed.

His father's silence told it all. The father had stolen; the boy had not.

My heart swelled. These men needed my help. Things came together.

Golden ore!

It explained all the secrets in the small town. Someone, a farmer most likely, had found a vein of it. The Jackal and his enforcers got word of it and took over the town. It wasn't the first time such things had happened, and it wouldn't be the last, either. Golden ore, however, wasn't gold, and it wasn't ore. It was a vein of mystic dirt that had a goldish hue to it.

"I'm hungry, Father. Do you think we'll eat again?"

Pitiful. I could make out the young man's face pressed against the bars. He was rawboned and lanky. Looked like he'd missed one too many meals already. It infuriated me, but the thought of action just made me sicker.

"Sure, Son. Sure we will," the father lied.

Don't think about it. Think of a way out. I allowed my thoughts to drift to the Golden Ore.

Farming was a big deal in Nalzambor. The land was rich, full, lustrous in many places. But working the land was still hard. It took time and a lot of work. And, in the case of hard work, many peoples and races were lacking. That's where the Golden Ore came in. Or, more simply called, Magic Dirt. A few pounds of it would turn a square mile of desert into a garden of vegetables. It was a pricey commodity, and it seemed the Enforcers had happened upon it.

But what did they want with me and these two men?

My voice was dry and raspy, but I managed to say, "I can get you out of here."

Both men stiffened and huddled down.

"I said, I can get you out of here."

The young man started to speak.

"Don't talk to him, Son. He might be that demon the innkeeper spoke of."

"I'm not a demon; I'm a man, same as the two of you," I said. *Sort of...* "Now, do you want help or not? Ugh!" I slunk onto the cage floor. My stomach was killing me. I needed healing.

"What happened?" the young man asked, pressing his face against the bars.

"Son, be quiet!"

"No." The young man was adamant. "I won't be. Sorry, Father. That man over there is offering help, and we need it!"

"But, I just—"

"I'm a man as well as you, Father. I'll live with the consequences of my actions."

I made it back to my knees and said, "Good for you. Now, tell me, how many of these enforcers are there?"

"I'm not sure, but there's a lot of them."

"Thirty-Seven," the father said.

He'd turned to face me now. Unlike his son, he was a barrel-chested man. The torchlight reflected dimly from the top of his head.

"How many of you in the village?"

"Almost a thousand," the father said.

Accounting for women and children, that didn't leave enough men to fight off a group of well-armed men. Fear doesn't wait long to rule.

"How long have they been here?"

"A few months. They showed up two days after we found the vein of Golden Ore. All the celebrating would have woke the dragons up. It's no wonder they showed up so fast with all the blabber mouths in this village."

I'd seen it happen before. If you didn't hire a well-armed force, the goons would quickly take over. Greed and treachery grew like weeds in Nalzambor. Better act quickly, before the roots got deep.

"And the Jackal? Where does he stay?"

I needed to find out where my gear was. It was the only way.

"He lords it over everyone in the day and diminishes in the night. He's wicked."

"He's crafty," the father added. "Dangerous. Something very strange about that fellow."

I'd sensed it, too. Something behind the man's eyes was raw, primeval.

The men jerked in their cages as the barn door slid open. Renny and Brock stepped inside, along with some of the other enforcers.

"Cover them cages," Renny said.

"What if they scream?" Harvey said.

"Oh yes, we can't have that, can we? Alright, gag these two, but the demon over there, he'll need more of the poison. Shoot him up, Brock!"

I could barely move already when Brock came, a sharp stick in one hand, a vial of Uken poison in the other. He dipped the stick in the ointment, laughing.

"Be still, Freak! Else I'll poke it in your eye."

I remained still. He stabbed through the bars. I tried to dodge, but caught the full force in my dragon arm.

"Did you stick him good?" Renny said.

"Real good."

I didn't hear anything else after that as my imprisoned world faded away.

CHAPTER
12

THE WAGON LURCHED TO A stop, and I awoke. It was still dark, but I knew I was outside because the breeze rustled the cover over my cage. Depressed and sick, I had a good idea how my brethren dragons felt. I had to escape, but I needed help.

"Almost time."

It was Renny, the leader of the Enforcers. Footsteps were all around, and I could also hear footsteps going up and down.

"Take the covers off. The Jackal will be here any moment, with company. Look sharp! Especially you, Osclar!"

Where was I? I felt the bump on my arm where Brock had jabbed me. It wasn't as bad as the one on my neck. I think the dragon scales had something to do with that. It had been more of a reflex than anything else when I made him hit my dragon arm. I hadn't meant for that, but maybe my arm had. And my head was a little more clear than before.

"Get over here, Harvey! Let's take this cover off and get started. Heh-Heh! Won't be long now before the fun starts."

Fun for him, maybe. Fun for me? I didn't think so.

"Sure thing, Boss. Sure thing."

The first thing I saw was the moon peeking through the clouds. Then I could smell the Enforcers' rancid breath.

"Huh, he's awake," Renny said, rubbing his chin. "Not sure the Jackal will like that. Harvey, let him know."

"Alright," Harvey said, strolling off.

I was inside a wooden fort, but I had a feeling it was designed to keep people in rather than out. Catwalks ran twelve feet high from one corner to the other. Enforcers with spears and swords guarded every corner and the space in between.

"Welcome to our Arena, Demon," Renny said. "The final resting place for you and many others on Nalzambor."

I locked my eyes on Renny and said, "And possibly yours as well."

He stiffened, said, "We'll see about that," and walked away, casting one glance back.

Entertainment! That's what I was. I remembered

the blazed ruffie battling the trolls. It turned my stomach, the cruelty of men.

"Go ahead and take those other two out," Renny ordered his men.

The farmers were pulled from their cages and the cages pulled away.

"Alright everyone. Get up on the wall. It's time for the battle to begin."

The father and son shook at each other's side.

"Please! Mercy enforcers! At least spare my son. I'm the guilty one!" the father begged.

The son looked at his father, a sad look in his eyes as he said, "You stole, Father?"

The father shook his head and replied, "Son, they stole from us. It's our land and our Golden Ore. These vultures have no right to take what is ours."

The Enforcers tossed down two shields and two clubs.

"I don't know how to fight, Father."

"Neither do I, Son." He hugged his boy. "I guess we'll have our first and last one together," the father said, picking the weapons up.

"Together then."

Renny shouted from above.

"That's the spirit!"

"Here he comes, Renny," Harvey said, looking over the backside of the wall.

The Jackal emerged from behind a wall and

stepped onto the catwalk. My sword Fang hung at his hip. My breast plate armor adorned his chest. My bow. My quiver and my pack. Infuriated, my heart thundered in my chest.

But he was different. His face was no longer that of a man, but an animal's. A Jackal's.

"I see everything is in order," The Jackal said, yellow eyes glowering at me. "I see our guest is bright eyed and bushy tailed. No matter." He fingered his claws over my sword. "Nothing I can't handle if need be."

A were-jackal. Another cursed man, like myself, but more like Corzan: corrupted by the evil. I felt a sliver of fear inside as I wondered if they'd both been good men once. I wondered what was in store for me. I rubbed the white spot of scales on my hand and vowed to do more good, given the chance.

"Farmers!" the Jackal yelled, the moonlight shining brightly on his face, "the time has come that you paid for your deceit. I told you when I came: what's yours is mine and mine alone, yet you stole. You sought to warn my enemies. And now you must pay."

The father and son trembled. Nalzambor was full of wonders, but I was certain they'd never seen a were-jackal before. Lycanthropes were evil. And there were plenty of stories and legends about them tearing people limb from limb. I could only imagine what was going through their minds at this moment.

"It's not much sport, is it?" I managed to say.

All eyes were on me. *Good*.

"But, I guess this is how cowards play," I added.

The Jackal leaned on the rail and smiled, his sharp teeth dripping in the moonlight.

"Oh, the do-gooder speaks. Interesting. And I can only assume you are going to talk and talk until it's over. Well then, I'll let the games begin. Enforcers, have at them."

Renny, Harvey and Osclar climbed down the ladders, while two more posted themselves at the top. The farmers readied themselves as more clubs and shields were tossed down from above.

Renny picked up his club and twirled it in the air.

"This won't take long. Watch my back, fellas."

The farmers shuffled back.

"Come on; take a swing," Renny said, sticking his chin out. "I'll give you a free shot."

The father's swing sailed over Renny's head.

Renny walloped him in the stomach, doubling him over.

The son caught Renny in the shoulder.

"Ow! You two idiots! I said to watch my back!"

Harvey and Osclar attacked, swinging hard and fast at that young man. The son gathered himself behind his shield, but they beat it down.

Wham! Wham! Wham!

The son folded like a tent.

Rushing to his son's aid, the father screamed, "NOOOOOO!" He huddled over his son, but the blows kept coming. I felt sick in my stomach when the men stopped, laughed, and walked off. There was nothing worse than seeing the work of evil first hand.

"Excellent, men!" the Jackal said. "Now that the warm-up is over, it's time for the real fight to begin. It's time to see how tough our visitor truly is. Let him out!"

CHAPTER 13

RUN! THAT'S WHAT I NEEDED to do. But not without my gear. And I couldn't abandon these people. I had to do what I had to do: stand up and fight for what's right.

I took my time getting out of the cage. My limbs were sluggish, and my head was full of mud. But I could move at last, and maybe I had my dragon heart to thank for that. Father had said it could do wonderful things.

Above, the Jackal stood, arms folded over his chest, all of my gear in place. It made me wonder if I was looking in a mirror. If that was what I would become if I didn't get my act together, then I had better try, and fast. Dark, primal, animal. That's what Corzan had called me, an animal. The Enforcers had said I was a freak and a demon. Sorrow and anger mixed in my stomach as I reflected on all I'd done wrong over the years. Holding my stomach, I shuffled forward and glowered up at him.

"I'll be needing my gear back, Lycan!" I said.

He sneered at me. They didn't' like that word, Lycan. But I didn't like the words Demon, Freak or Animal.

"I didn't come here to entertain your talk," he barked. "I came to watch you die. Take him!"

Clubs raised, Renny, Harvey and Osclar came at me.

Stomach in knots, weaponless, and with a dizzy head, I forged into battle.

I jumped over the three of them and darted for the farmers. They breathed, barely. I wrapped my fingers around both of their clubs, banged them together, and said, "Come and get me!"

They stopped, eyes wary.

"Fools! Take him!"

They screamed as they charged.

I cracked Renny in the jaw. Osclar in the head. Harvey in the knee.

Three down. Ten to go.

I smacked the clubs together and said, "Who's next!"

A wave of nausea assailed me, and I sank to my knee. The more active I was, the more the poison attacked my system. *Drat!* I had to fight it. I had to make my body do what it did not want to, or I was going to die.

I rose to my feet.

"Get the swords!" the Jackal yelled. "And get in there. You. You. You and You!" All the enforcers eyed the Jackal.

I smiled. All I needed was a blade. I could cut them to ribbons. They knew it.

"No! Just use clubs. And more men. You! You! You!"

They scrambled down, clubs and bucklers ready. That battle with the first three had taken a lot out of me. *Suck it up, Dragon!*

They came.

I swung.

They swung.

Back and forth we went, them chasing me from one side of the fort to another. I dodged, poked and parried. Where one fell, another popped up. A hard shot on my back knocked me to my knees. I ducked under the next swing, clubbed one in the chest, another in the knee.

Hard wood cracked. Shields smacked. Alarm and pain cried out.

I took a shot in the back of my head and pitched forward.

Whop! Whop! Whop! Whop! Whop!

They beat me like a drum.

I roared out.

"His eyes!" one said, backing off.

"He's a demon!"

A spark. A fire. An inferno came. My head cleared. My muscles loosened. I could see my reflection in the nearest man's eyes. My own eyes flared briefly with life. The effects of the poison fizzled out.

I cracked the clubs together.

"Let's try this again."

They ran. I pummeled.

I caught one in the chin. One in the nose. One in the jaw.

I laughed. It felt good to laugh and swing. Torment those crueler things. A minute later, not one man stood except me.

I looked up at the Jackal and said, "So, what happens when you run out of men?"

"I'm not concerned about that. Get in there, Brock!"

Brock, all eight feet of him, hopped down into the arena like a big ape. Well armored, he carried a spiked mace with a round head in one hand and a heavy chain in the other. When he stretched his arms out, it looked like they stretched from one side of the fort to the other.

"I see you've grown since we last talked," I said.

His lip curled over his teeth as he came forward.

"My, what an awfully long stride you have. Have you been eating Golden Ore? It's dirt you know. Is that why you grew so big?"

Swack!

I ducked as the chain licked out over my head.

His mace rose up.

His mace came down.

I dove away.

"I'm going to turn you into a mud hole," Brock said.

The mace and chain were like toys that he wielded like a child. A vicious child. The kind who plucks the wings off fairies.

He charged. I ran. He swung. I dodged. I ducked. I dived.

I could hear the Jackal's high-pitched laugh. Evil, condescending. I cast him a quick glance. He was twirling one of my Moorite arrows in his clawed fingers.

Brock's chain whipped around my legs and jerked me from my feet. I rolled as his spiked mace came down, clipping my arm.

"You're as big as you are inaccurate—Goon!" I said, whacking him in the hand.

He roared, releasing the chain. His mace came down, and rolling over the ground I went, kicking the chain from my feet.

"You are going to die!"

Brock swung.

I blocked. The impact of his hit jolted my elbows and ripped one club from my hand. The next blow was fast. I ducked. Brock knocked a small hole in the wall.

"What!" he cried out. The mace was stuck in the wall.

I swung the club full force into his elbow.

Brock howled like a banshee. I cracked one of his knees, then the other. Down on his knees he went. Tears filled his eyes as he screamed.

"Stop! Please stop it!"

I did not. Evil never showed me any mercy, so why should I show it?

I struck fast.

Whack!

Hard.

Whack!

On the final blow, I used both arms.

CRACK!

Brock fell face first into the ground. A red lump on his bald spot quickly formed.

Chest heavy, I said, "How's that treat you, Knothead!"

Above, the remaining enforcers gawked.

"Who's next?" I said, twirling my club around my back and front.

Every hair on my body lurched. *Move, Dragon!*

I felt my back catch fire as I spun to the ground, wounded, bleeding.

The Jackal loomed above me. Fang glimmered in his hand.

"You fight well against mortals. But you'll die against the power of the supernatural!"

Chapter

14

A PREDATOR. A TORMENTOR. THE JACKAL was a towering figure. Broad shouldered, strong and supple. An animal with the cunning of a man, the killer instinct of an animal. And Fang dangled in his evil grip. I never would have imagined I'd die on my own sword's blade. Backpedaling, I danced, and the lycan's swift strokes licked at my skin.

"You are fast for a big man," the Jackal said. "But, not as fast as me. I have supernatural speed. Skill. I'm your superior in battle!"

I laughed.

"You call this a battle? You wield a fine sword, and I use a club. Ha! You're letting my weapon and my armor do all of your dirty work, you over-sized rodent!"

"There is no honor among jackals!" he said, talking a swipe at my gut.

I jumped away.

"Or lycans, for that matter."

The walls of the fort were closing in, and the Jackal was quite a sight as four feet of razor sharp steel hung in his fist. My steel that is.

"It's sad to see your men are so much braver than you. At least they had the courage to fight with what they had, not with what the enemy had given them.

Fang sliced the top off my club. *Drat!*

I snatched a shield from the ground.

Wang!

The Jackal struck, jarring my bones. Again and again he tore at my shield, making pieces of metal and wood scatter all over.

"Coward!" I yelled. "Fight fair! What are you scared of?"

Krang!

"Your men are watching you. When the day comes, what will they think of you?"

Chop!

Only the straps and a small strip of wood remained. "Will they respect you? Will they follow?"

The Jackal stopped. I fought for my breath. He was little winded.

"I tire of your mouth. Perhaps it's best that I tear your throat out."

With a flick of his wrist, he tossed Fang to the other side of the fort. He stretched out his arms and extended the long nails on his fingers. I'd never fought a lycan, but I once saw one break the neck of a dwarf with his bare hands before. And there wasn't much that would kill a lycan except the pierce of silver or magic. I'd bought some time, but I was still a dead man without Fang.

"You'll wish I used the sword soon enough, Fool," he growled at me. "Now I'm going to tear you to pieces!"

Claws and teeth bared, he sprang. I dropped on my back, jammed my boots in his gut, and launched him head over heel. He crashed to the ground and howled. Not like I would, but with the strange high-pitched howl of a jackal.

He gathered himself, eyes filled with rage, and came again. Legs and arms ripping up the ground like an animal. I braced myself.

Slam!

I gave it all I had. I punched, kicked and clawed.

He bit, ripped and howled.

Blood was in my face. My blood, not his; I was sure of it. I walloped him in the jaw with my dragon fist, snapping his head back. I drove the heel of my other palm in his gut.

He backed off, smiled, and spit a tooth from his mouth.

"That's a first. But you bleed. I do not. I cannot."

I'd hit him with all I had with that punch. A dragon punch, at that—to no effect. That was the problem with the supernatural. Only the supernatural could stop it or kill it.

"You sure you just don't want to talk about this, Perhaps?"

He jumped again, his full weight landing on me. He rammed my face in the dirt and jammed a claw in my leg.

I thrashed. Drove an elbow in his ribs and rammed my head under his chin, crawling out from under him.

He shook it off like water and punched me in the face. My nose started to bleed. It might have been broken.

"I can do this all day," I said.

"Do what? Bleed? WHHHHH-HEEEEEEEEEOOOOOOO!" he howled like a tormented banshee. "We'll see about that!"

I had to fight smarter. Fight harder. Or else I'd be dead in the next minute. I gasped for breath. *Think, Dragon! Think! How do you beat something that is indestructible?*

I balled up my dragon fist and said, "Come on. What are you waiting for?"

He came after me, claws striking like snakes.
Jab! Jab!
I hit him in the nose.
Jab! Jab!

I hit him in the face.

He was fast, but my jabs were must faster. I was the dragon. He was the animal, not me.

He broke it off.

"What are you doing, Fool! You're can't hurt me!"

"Stings, don't it?" I shook my fist. "You might as well surrender. I can do this all night, remember."

I was exhausted, and my knuckles ached. The Jackal was like hitting a statue, but at least I had him aggravated.

Balling up his fists, he circled me.

"So it's a fist fight you want?" He smacked his together. "Then it's a fist fight you'll have."

He lunged.

I jabbed.

He snared my wrist in his hands.

"Gotcha!"

He jerked me to the ground and drove his elbow into my gut.

All my wind left me. The Jackal had outsmarted me. Pinned to the ground, I couldn't move. I couldn't breathe.

He opened his jaws.

I could see a tunnel of fangs in his mouth. I tucked my chin down as he went for my neck. *NO!* My mind screamed, but I knew it was over.

An inch from my face, the Jackal stiffened. His grip loosened. His jaw fell open. I noticed the tip of a sword sticking out of his chest as I crawled out from underneath him. His eyes rolled up in his head as he fell over.

Fang hung in the farmer's son's grip.

I scurried to my feet and watched the Jackal transform from lycan to man, dead.

The farmer's son stood there, trembling, with blood on his hands. I didn't know what to say, but the remaining Enforcers did.

"Kill them!"

CHAPTER 15

"**L**ET ME HAVE THAT," I said, holding out my hand.

"Oh," the son said, handing Fang over.

The metal was warm, welcoming, an old friend returned from a long trip.

The enforcers, five of them in all, surrounded us. A few others I'd knocked down before began to stir.

"I'll handle this," I said, twirling Fang around my body. Fang's radiant blade flared with light, a mix of many hues.

All the Enforcers gaped, eyes filled with wonder and fear.

"The Jackal is dead. Your leader's defeated. Do you want to be the first to taste my steel?" I said, pointing Fang at the nearest one. He cringed. "Would you rather die, or surrender?"

All the enforcers looked at one another and dropped their arms.

"Excellent. You soft bellies are not as stupid as you look. Now get in those cages."

They hesitated.

"Now!"

"We're going. We're going. We just weren't sure which one," one said, with shifty eyes and a black bandana on his head.

I gathered my pack, grabbed a healing vial, and applied a few drops to the young man's father's lips. He was barely breathing, but he coughed and sputtered.

"He's going to be alright," I said, extending my hand to the young man. "And I thank you. I owe you my life. That was a brave thing you did, you know?"

His chest swelled, and he couldn't help but smile as he grabbed my hand and squeezed it. He had a strong grip for a skinny fellow.

"I don't know what came over me. I didn't even think. I saw the Jackal tearing into you. The sword caught my eye, and I was moving." There was a watery twinkle in his eyes. "I've never wanted to kill anything before. Except food that is. But, I-I killed a man." He cast a look where the Jackal lay.

I squeezed his shoulder and said, "No, you killed a monster. You saved me. Your father. Yourself—and freed your village. One single act of bravery can yield great things."

Tears streamed down his cheeks as he helped his father to his feet.

"S-Son, what happened here?" the father said, looking around, a bewildered look in his weary eyes.

"Come on, Father. I'll tell you all about it on the way home." He stopped and looked at me, saying, "What is your name?"

"Call me Nath. Nath Dragon."

"Odd name, but memorable."

I smiled and asked, "What's yours."

"Ben."

"A fine name, Ben. A warrior's name."

"I'll be back with help."

I gathered my armor from the Jackal's corpse. All the stitching and buckles were fine, but Fang's tip had gone straight through the armor. A normal blade couldn't have done such a thing. It would be a little something for Brenwar to stitch up. *I bet he's ready to kill me.*

Gathering all my gear, I made my way up the ladders and onto the catwalk. I had no idea where I was. Horses nickered along the wall, a good sign.

The fort was erected on fertile land, between the rolling hills that stretched out mile after mile. Ben and his father traveled on horseback on a faint road that winded out of sight. I had a feeling it would be hours before I saw anyone else again, which left me and my prisoners, the Enforcers.

I looked at the men crammed in the cages. They were rotten. Every last one of them. How many people had they terrorized? How many had they killed? If I could have killed them in battle, I would have.

"And to think, all I wanted was a good meal and a warm night's sleep. Now what?"

I would be hours before anyone else came around, and I wasn't going to wait. I had dragons to save.

I said to Fang, "I guess it's me, you and the outdoors from now on." I slid him back in the sheath and hopped off the catwalk onto the ground.

"Let us go, Demon."

It was the leader, Renny, who spoke.

"We'll ride out of here and never look back. I promise."

Ignoring him, I grabbed the cloth and threw it over the cage.

"We can't see! You can't do that! It'll get too hot in here."

"And you will all begin to stink really bad, too. You better hope the gnolls and orcs don't get wind of you."

95

I covered the other two cages as well, laughing at all their colorful complaints.

"It smells like an orcen bathhouse in here!"

"Please don't leave us!"

"We're sorry! We won't raid any villages no more!"

"Oh no!" one moaned, "Brock just farted."

I was bound for Quintuklen. And I wasn't alone this time, either. I took the finest horse the Enforcers had, a big brown beauty. I rubbed his neck.

"No hurry, Boy. No hurry."

I found horses the most fascinating and noble of all the animals. Noble, strong and reliable. If you ever get a chance to know one or ride one, I suggest you do.

North I rode. Past the trees, through the ferns, over the streams from sun up until almost sun down.

"Wait!"

I heard someone crying out in the distance. Behind me, a man galloped waving a rag shirt or something in the air. It was Ben. Something must be wrong.

He came along side me, panting for breath.

"Your horse should be panting, not you." I said. "What's going on? Did the enforcers escape?"

"No, no!" he managed. "That's fine. The legionnaires are coming to haul them off."

"And you rode all this way to tell me that?"

He looked at me funny.

"No. I'm here because I'm coming with you!"

Chapter 16

"No, you aren't coming with me!" I said.

"Why not?" he said, grinning ear to ear.

Now it was my turn to gape. The young man was bruised from head to toe with a big knot on his head. He'd almost died hours ago, and now he wanted to follow me to a certain death.

"Because you'll die."

There, I'd said it. He'd just have to get over it. He frowned.

"Ben, be realistic. You stabbed a monster in the back. It died. And you have my sword to thank for that, else you'd never have scratched his hide."

He brushed his black hair behind his ear and said, "I never really thought about it."

"What you did was as I said. Brave. 'Bravery is for the foolish', some say. But fortunate as well. Why don't you just go home and enjoy your days being the hero of the village? The man that saved the town. I'm sure the milk maids would love for you to stick around."

A pleasant smile formed on his face.

"I hadn't' thought about that, either. Do you really think they'll like me?"

"A handsome young hero like you? Hah! They'll swoon as soon as you enter the room."

He was eyeing the sky and rubbing his chin. I knew I had him thinking now. With excitement in his voice, he said, "No! I want to go with you, Nath Dragon."

I shook my head. *What has possessed this young man?*

"No, and I don't have a shovel with me, either."

"A shovel? What do you need a shovel for?"

I turned my steed and trotted away, saying, "To dig your grave. Goodbye, Ben. And tell the milk maids hello."

The clopping of horse feet were catching up. I turned.

"Ben, go home. I mean it!"

"But you owe me!"

"Owe you? For what?"

"You said, 'I owe you my life'. You can pay me back now."

Great! Ben had a point. I owed him my life.

Irritated, I said, "What do you want?"

"Uh, well, er... I just want to go with you. See the world. Travel Nalzambor."

Ben looked about as fit for travel as a one-legged horse. His trousers were held up by a rope belt, and the leather armor that he must have taken from an Enforcer was too big. His arms jutted out from under the shoulder plates like sticks, and the sword strapped to his waist looked like it would pull him from the saddle. He would have been the most pathetic enforcer I ever saw.

"Are you certain you want to do this, Ben?" I smiled.

Reason with him. Talk him out of it.

"Absolutely. More than anything. I don't want to work on the farm anymore. It's boring. I want to see the world."

"And you want to face all the dangers therein?"

"Well, I guess."

"You ever seen an ogre pull a man's arms off?"

"No."

"Have you seen a Chimera swallow a gnoll?"

"What's a Chimera?"

I rolled my eyes.

"Do you know there are goblins that eat people?"

"No."

"Orcs that enslave people?"

He shook his head.

"Fierce dragons that burn the living to a crisp?"

His eyes fluttered in his head. Then he said, "Oh... I'd love to see that!"

"Really?"

"Well, not good people. Just ones like the enforcers and all."

I could see a dangerous look in his eyes. A fire. A twinkle. A zeal. Ben wasn't going home. He was coming with me, on an adventure.

I sighed.

"Come on then. But I'll not feed you, clothe you or baby you. So, you better keep up."

His long face lit up like a halfling parade. "Really? You'll let me come!"

"It's your life to throw away, not mine."

"So it is," he said, grinning ear to ear. "Let's go!"

I led. He followed. Over the faintest of trails we went.

As the minutes passed and the sun set, Ben finally asked, "Er... Nath?"

"Call me Dragon," I scowled.

"Er... Dragon, where are we going?"

CHAPTER 17

"QUINTUKLEN, WHERE THE BUILDINGS ARE as tall as the Red Oak trees," I said. "But it's a long, long ride."

"I'm in no hurry," Ben replied, yawning.

Skinny as the young man might be, he had some grit to him. Underneath all the bruises, he probably wasn't a half-bad looking lad, either. He just needed to eat more. Dark-complexioned and tall, he was at ease in the saddle. His light eyes followed all the sights and sounds. And unlike Brenwar, he smiled and talked a good bit.

"Tired, Ben?"

"A good bit, actually. I haven't rested since being hauled off in that cage. Shouldn't we be making camp already? I can make a fire."

"What do you need a fire for? Didn't you bring a blanket?"

"No."

I shook my head.

"But I meant I could do some cooking. I'm a good hunter and trapper."

"I thought you were a farmer."

"Well, you can't survive in the country if you can't hunt or fish. You'll starve eventually."

As soon as the white owls began to hoot, I stopped in a grove and made camp, which consisted of little more than two horses and two men with a rough patch of ground to lie on. Ben yawned the whole time as he gathered twigs and started a fire. He did well. After a few minutes, the orange glow burst to life and the warmth came.

"Outstanding, Ben. You are pretty handy, are you not?"

Covering his yawn, he said, "I told you."

"Good, now you can take the first watch. Wake me up when the moon dips."

Ben had a blank look in his eyes.

"And keep your ears open. They'll serve you better than your eyes at night," I said, closing my eyes. I could feel Ben's eyes on my back as rubbed his hands on the fire.

"I'll stay awake, Dragon. All night if I have to."

I lay and listened. Chirps of critters and crickets filled my ears. All those little things that crept and crawled in the night had come to life. A burning fire offered sanctuary, but it could attract the unwanted. Good thing I was a light sleeper. And I had a sixth sense for danger. The Dragon's Gut, I called it. An awareness I had when I slept, though I didn't sleep much. As I drifted off to sleep, the soft snoring of Ben drifted into my ears.

"Oh great," I said, sitting up.

He lay alongside the fire, curled up in his armor.

"Looks like I have the first and the second watch."

The pixlyn flew as fast as he could fly, covering a mile a minute. Hummingbird wings buzzing as fast as they ever buzzed before. Over the tree tops he went, scattering insects and small birds. Little noticed him. Little could see him.

In a day, he'd covered the northern part of Nalzambor. He'd seen many faces in that day: dwarves, elves, orcs, giants and dragons, some hard at work or mischief, others at play. But there was yet to be a sign of the man he sought. Nath Dragon. He rubbed his belly, panting. The potion Finnius had given him was a nasty thing, like rotten stew boiling. It gave him strength somehow. A sense of direction, too. The man must be close. He could feel it.

He thought of his companion, the pink-eyed pixlyn he'd been with all his life. Find the man, save her. He couldn't bear the thought of horrible things happening to her. He took a deep breath in his tiny mouth, stuck out his chest and buzzed into the sky.

A streak of red came at him. He rolled away, hovering in the sky. There were three of them. Each was as big as him, red-scaled and black-winged, tiny dragons called firebites. They circled, snorted puffs of fire, and dove.

The pixlyn shot through the sky, three dangerous dragons nipping at his toes. Firebites didn't play with pixies and fairies. They roasted them and ate them whole.

The pouring rain didn't bother him. Nor the stubborn horse between his legs. No, as Brenwar trotted along the road, he was consumed with something else. Guilt.

"I should have listened to him," he growled, wringing the water from his beard.

He had known Nath wanted to leave Morgdon, and Brenwar should have gone. Instead, being stubborn, persistent and consumed with the Festival of Iron, he might end up losing his best friend. And it might end up starting another war. Not that Brenwar would mind that. But he had to catch him. And catching Nath wouldn't be easy. Not if he didn't want to be found.

Another Dragon War, Nath's father had warned. That's what evil wanted. Another shot at the throne of Nalzambor. Nath's father, the Dragon King, wasn't the same as he had been of old. Not after the last war. He was ancient, but not immortal. Brenwar sensed that the Dragon King's time on Nalzambor was coming to an end. And who would keep the peace without him there? It was either Nath Dragon or no one.

The horse nickered and stopped.

"What is it now?" Brenwar said, rubbing its neck.

A group of figures approached, cloaked from head to toe. Men, by the looks of them.

"Hail and well met," one said, fingers itching at the sword on his hip.

"Agreed," said another who stepped behind Brenwar's back.

As easy as a fish swims in water, they had him surrounded.

Brenwar stiffened as the next one said, "That's a fine horse you have there, Little Dwarf."

Whop!

Brenwar knocked him out of his boots with his war hammer.

"Little! I'll show you brigands little!"

Brenwar slid from his horse to the ground.

"Take him down!" one ordered, drawing his sword.

Two rushed forward. Brenwar busted one in the

chest, dropping him in the mud. The other stabbed a dagger into his armored chest, snapping it at the hilt.

"Fool! This armor's dwarven made!"

"Drag him into the mud!" one of the brigands said.

Brenwar took in a loud draw through his nose.

"Ah, I smell an orc, a part of one at least."

Brenwar knocked a curved sword from one's hand. Kicked in the knee of another. He was a machine. A black bearded typhoon in the rain.

A man screamed as he busted his hand. Another fell as his knee gave out. One caught Brenwar in the back of his leg with a knife.

"You should not have done that!" he said, swinging his war hammer.

Pow!

He lifted the man's feet from the ground.

The rain poured. The brigands tumbled down. No group of Brigands stood a chance against a dwarven soldier with centuries of fighting under his belt.

Brenwar grabbed the fallen half-orc by its head of hair and said, "Happen to see a man with long auburn hair and golden eyes pass through here, Wart Face?"

"I wouldn't say if I did, Halfling. Heh-heh!"

"Why is it the ugly ones always have the smartest mouths!"

"Because—"

Brenwar clonked his head into the orc's, knocking him out.

"That was a statement, not a question. Now, what about the rest of you?"

"Mercy, Sir," one said, clutching his broken arm. "Never seen such a man. If I did, I'd tell you. I swear."

"Sure you would," Brenwar said, hoisting himself back on his horse. "If I ever see any of you again, I'll break every bone in ya!" He snapped the reigns. "Yah!"

Aggravated, Brenwar felt he wasn't any closer to finding Nath Dragon than when he started. But he was certain time was running out.

Chapter 18

"SLEEP WELL?" I SAID.

Ben stretched out his arms and yawned.

"What happened!" he said, covering his eyes. "Where'd all this daylight come from?"

"I'm pretty sure it's from the sun," I said, roasting a rodent on a spit. "It does that most days, you know."

"I'm sorry. I didn't mean to fall asleep. I felt just fine, then I was out." Ben's stomach growled. "What's that you're cooking? Smells good."

"Just a little white-eared rabbit."

"Really? How'd you snare it? We can never keep them out of the garden. Too smart for snares, too fast to shoot."

I held out another rabbit on the end of my arrow.

"I shot this one, too," I said.

"Nobody's that good a shot," Ben objected. "Not even my uncle. He's a Legionnaire bowman, you know. He told me they could hear me pulling the string back before I shot." He tore a hunk of meat off the stick. "Hmmm... this is good. Really good!"

"Well, I'm sure your uncle is a fine shot. And the white-ears are impossible targets. You just have to know where to shoot before they go. It's called 'anticipation'. And, I had a little help, too."

I held Akron out.

"What is that?"

Snap-Clatch-Snap!

"Whoa," he said when the bowstring coiled along the bow and into place. "Is that magic?"

"No, all bows do that."

"Really?"

"Of course not. This is Akron. A gift from my father. Elven made. Elven magic. Can you shoot?"

"Can I shoot? You bet I can shoot. My uncle started teaching me when I was just a boy. I once shot a sparrow in the sky. I feathered a boar, too. Right between the eyes. It was him or me, that time." He licked the rabbit meat from his fingers. "Can I try?"

Ben rose up, twisted and cracked his back. His eyes were alert, and the rangy muscles throughout his body were supple, not stiff. If he had some armor that fit, he'd actually look like a soldier, and the fact that his uncle was a Legionnaire archer left me a little more comfortable. I handed over the bow and an arrow.

"*If*," I emphasized, "you can pull the string back, let it fly." I pointed. "That oak tree will do."

Ben took the grip in his hand, loaded the shaft on the shelf, and nocked it back like a seasoned soldier. Arms quivering, he pulled the fletching to his cheek.

"Hold it steady, Ben."

He took a small breath, held it, steadied his aim, and released.

Twang!

The arrow sailed with speed and accuracy.

Thunk!

"Yes!" Ben pumped his arm. "This bow is amazing!"

"That's a great shot, Ben. You're pretty strong for a scrawny man," I said, taking my bow back. "You were a little low, however."

The tree was thirty yards off, but I couldn't have him getting cocky.

"I don't think many men could do much better."

I loaded Akron, pulled the string back, and let one arrow fly after the other.

Twang! Thunk!
Twang! Thunk!
Twang! Crack!

The first hit above Ben's, the second below. The third went right through his shaft.

"Uh, that was amazing!"

"Of course it was," I said handing him my bow.

"Can you teach me to do that?"

"Probably not, but..." I eyed the heavy sword on his belt, thinking. "Ever swing a sword before?"

"Just the once. My mother didn't like weapons, and my father didn't care for them much, either."

"Well, if you have to use it, better try it two-handed. I'll show you a few things later. Now run down there and fetch those arrows."

Ben started walking towards the tree.

"I said *Run*!"

He sprinted for the tree. *At least he's fleet.*

Looking backward, the pixlyn wiped the sweat from his brow. The skies were empty. His pursuers gone. The firebites, who in comparison to him, for all intents and purposes, might as well have been full-sized dragons, had chased him until it felt like his wings would fall off. He zipped down into the trees and took a seat on a branch behind the leaves. He'd never flown so much in one day before.

Chest heaving, he frowned as he thought of his companion: her beautiful pink eyes and sweet smile. Even if he returned with what the evil man wanted, he knew they were both still dead. But it was better they died together, rather than separate.

They'd lived for one another. They'd die for one another. That's what love is.

He shuddered as he thought of the firebites. He could only guess they had tired out or found the scent of easier prey. As for the rest of the journey, he'd have to be more careful. No doubt they would pursue if they found the scent again. He shivered, mumbling in Pixlyn to himself. He rubbed his belly. The strange aching had grown stronger. He could sense the man he'd been sent to track was getting closer. His toes lifted off the branch as his wings hummed to life, and he darted off. His neck whipped around at the sound of tiny dragons roaring.

Zip!

Into the night, he was gone.

CHAPTER
19

T HE NEXT COUPLE OF DAYS occurred without
incident, and I was relieved. Ben had a strong
core, and after a few lessons, he could swing
his sword like a weapon. He was pretty adept for
a long-leg with skinny arms, but working on the
farm will do that to you. The problem with most
farmers being soldiers was the only weapons they
wielded were pitchforks, hoes and buckets of slop.

"Slash, Ben!" I said, banging his sword away.
"Don't poke. Don't stab. That sword's not made for
that. You need a light, smaller sword if you want to
stab. And a quick opponent will roll right past you
and slash your arm off. Have you ever seen a man
poke a man's arm off before?"

Ben shook his head.

"If you poke them, they might bleed, but slash
a part off, and they'll run."

Ben's face tightened.

"Hard to imagine such a thing, but when you fight, these things happen. They can happen to you just the same." I slapped him on the shoulder. "But this *is* what *you* wanted, isn't it?"

He looked a little green as he shook his head yes.

"But stabbing's how I killed the Jackal," he said, thumbing notches on his blade's edge.

"True, but the Jackal wasn't looking—and you had a magic sword, to boot." I twirled Fang with my wrist. "He's a fine thing, isn't he?" I rubbed the dragon heads on the pommel then jerked Dragon Claw out for display. "Now, if you want to poke somebody, you need one of these."

"Whoa! I never would have imagined such a thing," he said, eyeing it with fascination.

"This is Dragon Claw, and he's helped me out of more than one jam or two. When we get closer to town, well find you a dagger for your boot." I tugged at his girdle. "Hmmm, probably can fit a nice one in there, as well. You can never be too careful."

As Ben rubbed the back of his neck, I could see the uncertainty build in his eyes. *Good. A young man like that needs to know what he's in for.* But I was going easy on him, for now.

"I'm hungry."

"I'll check the fish traps," Ben said, sliding the broad sword into his belt.

"And I'll start the fire," I said.

I liked Ben. He was good company, and other than a few glances, he hadn't even asked about my arm, which I found extraordinary. But, country folk always did have the best manners.

After gathering a few twigs and skinning down some branches, I had a fire going in no time. It wasn't long after when Ben returned with a string of fish.

"Pretty nice catch you have there," I said.

He grinned from ear to ear.

"That stream is full of them. I could fish here all week."

I cooked; he skinned, and not long after I lay on my back and watched the wind blowing the black silhouettes of the leaves.

"Think you can stay up this time?" I said.

Ben covered his mouth, yawning.

"Oh, I'm feeling spry tonight." He grabbed a stone and ran it along the edge of his sword. "Dragon, I was wondering. What do you do, exactly? Do you hunt treasure? Where are you from? I've never seen a man like you before. And when I left, all the people were talking about you."

I sat up.

"Really, what did they say?"

"My cousin said you were one of those dragon poachers."

"Really," I held up my hand, "with an arm like this?"

He scratched his neck and said, "It is peculiar, but I've seen strange travelers before." He perked up. "I even saw some elves once. They didn't talk, but they had the most beautiful armor."

"Listen, Ben. If you're going to ride with me, and you might just die with me, you might as well know."

He leaned forward.

"Know what?"

"I'm looking for dragons."

His eyes brightened.

"You're a hunter?"

I shook my head.

He snapped his fingers.

"A poacher then? I've heard about them. Uh…" He shrank back. "…but aren't they… evil?"

"Yes, but I am neither. I don't hunt dragons. I don't kill them. I rescue them."

He scratched his head and asked, "Why would a dragon need rescued?"

"What do you know about the dragons, Ben?"

He shrugged.

"They have fiery breath and scales as hard as steel. Some are as big as horses and others as small as a goat." His face drew up. "Will you take me with you? To rescue one? Oh, they have treasure, too. Wagon loads of it, I hear. And… and there are thousands of them in the Mountain of Doom. They say there's one so large there he can swallow an elephant whole."

There was only one who could, that I knew of.

"Where'd you hear that?"

"A troubadour who was passing through one day sang about it. She was a pretty young thing. Half-elven she said she was, with honey-brown hair and lips the color of wine."

"And she sang no songs of auburn-haired fellows with eyes as gold as the sun?"

"No."

"Are you certain?"

"I'd have remembered for sure. We don't get many bards where I come from."

I rose to a knee, hand instinctively falling to my hilt.

"What is it?" Ben said.

I put my finger to my lips.

He cupped his ear.

What I heard was flapping. And not the common kind of the night air. Not birds, not owls, nor any other common thing, but something vastly rare.

The horses nickered. Their hooves stomped and stammered.

"Stay with the horses!" I said, pulling my bow out. "Something bad is coming."

CHAPTER

20

IT WAS BAD, ALRIGHT. THREE times as bad as I thought it would be.

"Firebites! What in Narnum are they doing here!"

Yes, they're dragons. No, they aren't good. Not evil, but not good. They're also known in the Dragon Home as firebrats.

I ducked.

A small creature zinged over my head. A pixlyn. A small fairy-like man with wings. A firebite was on his tail, chasing him into the sky, darting in and out of the trees. I could see two more waiting above as their brother flushed the pixlyn out.

"Ben! Don't leave those horses, do you hear?"

Firebites are small, little bigger than my foot, but they're all dragon. Nasty dragons, red-scaled, black-winged, more than capable of handling their own in the big, big world.

"What did you say?" Ben shouted back. "What are those things, anyway?"

"Stay with the horses, Ben!"

I nocked an arrow. Not moorite. Not magic. Just one I used for hunting. The pixlyn came again. I shot. He dove. The arrow splintered off the pursuing firebite's nose. It howled a split second before it crashed into a tree.

"Excellent shot, Dragon!"

"Get to the horses, Ben!"

In a blink, I reloaded, eyeing the sky. Down the next two came.

"Always have to do it the hard way, don't you fellas?" I said, aiming.

Twang!

The arrow split on its face. A normal arrow wouldn't harm it, but it would sting. I stepped out of the way as it crashed to the ground.

A stream of flame shot from the third one's mouth.

"What are you doing, Fire Brat?" I said, jumping away. The tree behind me burst into flame. If I didn't calm them down, they'd set the entire forest on fire. The next thing I knew, they had me surrounded. Vicious little lizards, tongues licking around their red hot mouths, snorting smoke and flames from their nostrils.

"Why are you attacking me?"

I felt something brush against my hair.

"Sultans of Sulfur!" I had a pixlyn on my head. "Get off me!"

The dragons' razor-sharp teeth nipped at my boots as they circled.

I could feel the white-hot heat coming out of their mouths. They could fry me in an instant if they wanted. I could see the fury in their eyes. They wanted that pixlyn.

I tried some Dragonese, saying, "Go away. The hunt is over."

They stopped and cocked their heads like little red dogs.

"Peace and Home," I said, and repeated.

Firebites are rebels. They come and go as they please. And they're harder to catch than most dragons. They don't have the weakness for gems or gold. It's the hunt and torment of all creatures inferior that they live for.

Sitting back on their haunches, they growled a little. Behind me, the burning tree was beginning to crackle.

"That's more like it," I said, reaching my dragon arm out to the nearest. It growled, bloodstone eyes fixed on my shoulder. There, the pixlyn sat, huffing for breath, a worried expression on his tiny face. The poor creature was exhausted. "You better stay back," I said. I felt it conceal itself in my locks.

"I'll help you, Dragon!"

From out of nowhere, Ben came swinging his sword.

"No, Ben! Stop!"

It was too late.

"EEE-YAH!"

Ben swung hard, hitting a firebite, sending it skipping across the ground.

"Fool! I told you to stay with the horses! Now we'll—"

A stream of flames shot from two dragons' mouths.

I leaped, knocking Ben out of the way.

"Stay behind me!" I said, locking my bow on my back. *Shing!* Fang was secure in my grip.

"Are those dragons?" Ben said, behind my ears.

"No, fool! Those are angry dragons! Very angry!"

"You sound angry," Ben said, worried. "Are you?"

I didn't say anything. Ben only meant well, but good intentions were often a brave man's undoing.

Puff! Puff! Puff!

Three balls of fire shot my way. I swatted them away with my sword, the splatter burning my fingertips and arms.

"Ow! That burns!" Ben said behind me.

Whatever connection I'd had with the firebites was gone now. Not only did they want the pixlyn, they now wanted Ben and me, as well. And these firebites were fully grown; their fire, though small, would last much longer than others'.

"What do we do?" Ben said. "I don't want to be burned alive."

I could feel Ben sliding away from me.

"Don't you dare run," I growled. "They'll turn you into char before you get within a dozen yards of a horse. Stand your ground and live. Give ground and die."

Nervous, Ben said, "That's what my uncle the Legionnaire says."

I didn't see any way out of this. They were going to hurt us, fry us, burn us. The intent was there as their tails snapped back and forth. They'd burn the entire forest down if they wanted to. I'd have to use Fang. I'd have to be quicker than them.

"Fang, if you have any advice, I could use it now."

"What?" Ben said.

"Nothing," I said. "Prepare yourself."

As Ben and I stood side by side, I saw the firebites' tiny chests swell. A torrent of flame shot out.

CHAPTER
21

INSTANTLY, A WALL OF ICE formed before me.
Fang's blade radiated an icy blue color, the like
I'd never seen on the metal before.

"Whoa!"

On the other side, the dragon flames crackled
against the ice, causing the sheet to melt. With
Fang glowing like a blue star in my hand, I seized
the moment.

"Stay behind this wall," I ordered Ben.

Fang was pulsating with power. It was
intoxicating. I stepped around the wall and faced
the tiny dragons. In Dragonese, I spoke.

"That's enough! Be gone, firebites!" I said,
pointing at them with my sword.

Fireballs shot from each mouth, pelting me
with fire.

"Argh!" I screamed. It hurt, but just like when

the steel dragon breathed fire on me, it didn't destroy me.

Fang moaned, angry, and blasted shards of ice into all of them.

Defiant, they let out with tiny roars, mouths shooting with fire.

Fang hit them again, coating them with frost from head to toe.

Growling, shivering, they backed away.

I willed Fang to shoot them again. The fire brats deserved it.

"Get out of here while you can!"

Wings pinned to their sides, one by one, they scampered away. The last one, looking back, shot another blast of fire my way. I ducked, and when I looked back, it was gone.

Still filled with power, I shot another blast into the burning tree. The ice smothered the flames out. Admiring Fang, I said, "That was incredible."

Fang flared and moaned, then returned back to his shiny coat of steel.

"Well done, Fang. And thank you," I said, sliding him back into his sheath.

I remembered what the steel dragon had said. *That sword you have, Little Dragon... you should get to know it better... that day your father forged it, I was there... tell him hello... and thank you.*

There was certainly much more to that than I expected.

"You talk to your sword," Ben said, stepping from behind the wall of ice, "And it makes snow?"

I fought the urge to slap him.

"Ben! You almost got us killed. Do you understand that?"

He stood there, blinking.

"Do you want to continue this journey with me?" I said, patting out a patch of flame on my armor. I had burn marks all over me, and a nasty boil popped up on my arm.

He nodded.

"Then, follow my orders from now on!" I punched him in the arm. "Got it!"

He grimaced, holding his shoulder.

I shrugged. That's what Brenwar would have done if I'd acted so foolish. I felt Ben eyeing my back.

"Were those dragons? They were so small."

"Yes, those were dragons. And as you can see, just because something is small, doesn't mean it's not dangerous. Take a moment to think: what would have happened if they came after you without me? You'd be a Human Roast, right? And they have our scent now. They might come back, you know. Burn us in our sleep."

Eyes like saucers, tone somber, he nodded and said, "I'm sorry, Dragon. I guess we're even, huh?"

"I guess—say what?" Something rustled in my hair. I'd forgotten about the pixlyn.

Snatch!

I had him in my dragon claws.

"What is that!" exclaimed Ben.

The pixlyn struggled in my grip, but I wasn't hurting him. I wasn't letting him go, either.

"A pixlyn, part of the fairy race."

Ben came closer, gaping, and said, "I heard they granted wishes."

I laughed but not out loud. *This should be good.*

"Go ahead, make a wish then," I suggested.

"Well, why don't you make a wish, then?"

I closed my eyes, thinking, and said, "Hmmm… well, I didn't really have one in mind, but if you're not interested, I could think of one; I guess. I'm hungry: maybe some food."

"No! Do something bigger than that."

"What would you wish for, Ben?"

This should be interesting. You could learn a lot about a person if you knew what they wished for.

Scratching the side of his cheek, looking between me and the fairy, Ben said, "I'd wish for peace in all Nalzambor."

Well, that was touching. Naïve, but at least his heart was in the right spot. *He'll make a fine hero yet.*

"Impressive, but pretty big, Ben. Their magic is limited, so you might as well ask for something smaller."

"Can I save it?"

"Sure, you can do whatever you want."

He glanced at me and said, "He can't really grant wishes, can he?"

"I can neither confirm nor deny that.

The pixlyn chattered at me, but I had no idea what he said. I imagine it was "Let me go!"

"What are you going to do with him?"

The pixlyn was an exotic and handsome little thing. His skin was the color of pollen, his eyes like tiny gems. A perfect figurine of a man. Still, it was strange to find a pixlyn so far from the high mountains. And I found it hard to believe the firebites rousted him out from there. And the creature, though defiant in my grasp, seemed sad, almost worried.

"What is wrong—"

A puff of blue smoke shot from his mouth and into my face, my mouth, my eyes.

Oh no! The lights went out, and my memories began to fade.

CHAPTER

22

I AWOKE WITH THE SUN IN my eyes and a headache.

"Ugh... what hit me?"

"Nothing," Ben said. "That fairy or pixie thing just spat on you."

I rolled over. There was Ben, glum-faced and dark-eyed. He looked like he hadn't slept in a week.

"You been up all night?"

He rubbed his eyes, yawning.

"Yep. I couldn't sleep if I had to. I swore I heard those little dragons prowling around all night." He huffed out a breath. "I'm really glad you're awake because I couldn't wake you, and I tried. Oy, did I try."

I sat up, looking around, rubbing my head. There was a lump on it.

"Sultans of Sulfur, Ben! Couldn't' you catch me when I fell? What did I land on, a stone?"

"Sorry, but I was watching that pix... er—"

"Pixlyn!" I growled. "So, I guess it's long gone by now. Hope you got your wish in. Now get the gear and the horses; let's go!"

I was agitated. It wasn't all Ben's fault, but having him around didn't help. It just slowed me down. I had dragons to save, and the only thing I was saving was myself and him. It was time to get him to the city and settle him in. I had things to do.

I saddled up as soon as Ben led the horses over.

"You get everything?" I asked.

"Certainly. Eh, Dragon?"

"What?"

"That blister on your arm, it looks painful. I could lance it for you. I saw my mother lance one on my father once. He burned himself really bad at the forge. A hot horse caught him."

The blister was as big as an egg and throbbed with a life of its own. A chronic reminder of my carelessness.

"Do I look like someone who's worried about a little blister on my arm?" I said, scowling. I didn't smile all the time, unless ladies were around.

"No."

I slit it open with my dragon thumb.

Ben looked like he'd swallowed a scorpion as the puss drained out.

"There, Ben. You don't have to worry about me anymore." I snapped the reigns. "Yah!"

Quintuklen. A monolithic marvel against the northern skies.

"What do you think?" I said.

Ben stared, saying, "I never imagined it was so big."

It was big. The biggest city in Nalzambor, which I always found odd, because humans didn't stick around as long as the rest of us. But they were an ambitions lot.

"How tall are those... those things?" Ben pointed.

"Those are called *buildings,* and they're the tallest structures in the world. Excluding the Mountains of course. Naturally."

Even I admired them. It was a fascinating view, from the top of one to the streets below. The people seemed so tiny. It made me long for flying once more.

We trotted along a road heading towards the city, which was still miles in the distance.

"Uh, Dragon?"

"Yes."

"I'm, well, I'm..."

I saw the lump in his throat roll up and down.

"Scared, I'd imagine."

He nodded.

"Don't worry, Ben. It's normal. And once we

get in there and see all the people, those fears will trickle away. Just don't buy anything or talk to the painted ladies. The merchants have a name for newcomers like you."

"A name? What kind of name?"

"Lilly pad. People will be nice, but too nice can be deadly."

He blanched.

"And if you have any money, keep it in your boots. There are pick pockets all over. Are you listening?"

"Oh… sorry, it's just those buildings. So big. I never could have imagined it."

"You'll get used to it. Now, stay close to me and don't smile. That only invites unwanted attention."

"Alright, Dragon."

The city, like all the rest aside from the Free City of Narnum, was fortified. A stone wall just over six feet tall was the first line of defense, but there were no gates or guards, just gaps spaced out every half mile or so. A hundred yards farther in, we came to the second wall: about twelve feet high with soldiers marching back and forth on the catwalks.

Looking around, I said, "Hold on." Reaching into my pack, I grabbed the Vial of concealment and dripped two drops on my dragon arm.

"What's that?" Ben said.

"Watch."

I thought of what I wanted. My black scales faded, and only my skin and fingers remained.

I wasn't so sure I liked it, but I didn't want any attention, either.

"Whoa!" Ben said. "Can that make me look different, too?"

Does he think potions grow on trees? "No," I lied, "It just conceals my scales. That's all I wanted. Come on, now."

Two massive wooden doors remained open, and we passed through with a throng of merchants and travelers, maybe an adventurer or two.

"Follow me," I said, "And don't stare at anybody."

Through a gap in the wall we went; into the city we came. Ben gasped from behind me. There were people everywhere. Women draped the windows of tiny apartments: whistling, smiling and carrying on. Pushy merchants shoved sticks of cooked meat in our faces.

"Try some. The best. Make you strong warriors!" an elder one said, flashing his gums.

"Stop that!" Ben cried.

A half dozen little children were pulling at his boots. He shoved one down and into the ground. All the children screamed and cried, "Soldiers! Soldiers!"

"Stick your boots in the stirrups and ride on, Ben," I said through my teeth. "Let's go."

"Halt!"

A group of well-armed soldiers were coming our way.

CHAPTER
23

EVIL GLEE ON HIS FACE, Finnius the Cleric slapped his hands together.

"Headed towards Quintuklen! My, that's perfect, maybe too perfect, but I'll take my chances. You've done well, Pixlyn, very well indeed."

The pixlyn stood back inside his cage, tiny hands wrapped around the bars, speaking shrill words of fairy kind. Along his side in her own cage, the female pixlyn sat, knees folded up in her arms.

"Certainly, I'll let you go," Finnius said, leering down at the cage. "I'll let you both go, just as soon as I'm... FINISHED WITH YOU!" He motioned for one of the acolytes. "Cover them both. I've no need of them at this moment."

The acolytes each dropped a heavy dark cloth over a cage and bowed their bald heads at Finnius.

He nodded. It wasn't so long ago that he was one of them. A lowly cleric, given a simple task of confronting Nath Dragon. He had a limp to show for it, but that was all it had taken. Selene was pleased with his success. He'd earned her trust, which was no small matter. Now he had the tattoos and greater power to show for it.

"Follow me," he said, leaving one chamber for another.

The temple rooms were an excellent sanctuary for evil. Tucked in the rocky folds of the hills east of Quintuklen, they didn't get many trespassers in the long-abandoned temple. It was easy to keep secrets that way. And the constant howl of the winds kept the staunchest adventurers away.

"Nath Dragon," he said, laughing a little, "falling right into our hands. The High Priestess will be pleased, pleased indeed."

Down a short set of stone steps he went, torches bristling in the stiff wind, leading them into a chamber of worship. The draykis hissed as he entered. The accompanying lizardmen stood at attention, spears crossed over their chests.

"At ease; I've news to share," he said, walking over to the cage of the yellow dragon they'd caught days earlier and squatting down. Eyes closed, it didn't budge an inch. "It seems our game is close. Close indeed, and if we plan and stay prepared, we can lead our prey right here."

"Just tell us where he is, Finnius," the winged draykis said. "We shall go and kill him."

The draykis towered over him, fists clenched at its sides, fiery eyes boring down on him.

Finnius's hand fell to the symbol of Barnabus that hung from his neck.

"Back up," he said, "and mind your distance, Creature."

"Hah, Mortal, don't be so certain that amulet will protect you. It's you who should show respect," it said, clutching the long claws on its fingers.

Unruly. The dead are so unruly. Finnius squeezed the amulet tight.

"Barnabus!"

A wave of dark and eerie light burst forth, knocking the draykis from their feet. The amulet shimmered, ebbed, then returned to form: two bronze dragon heads facing outward. Each different; both evil.

"I've been dying to do that," he said. "Now, as you can see, we have many prisoners that need protection."

Scowling, the draykis rose back to their feet, looking around.

Four cages were lined up along the walls of the worship chamber. The yellow streak, as big as a man, and three small dragons, each in a cage of his own. One White, the size of a cat, and two greens as big as dogs. The draykis made catching the dragons easy, and Finnius was astounded by their success.

"Finnius," one of the acolytes spoke up, a younger man in oversized robes, "the cages' enchantment ebbs. Shall I fetch the elements?"

"Certainly," Finnius said. "And you may handle it yourself. I can't have the dragons getting out, and a little more deterrent will help."

One dragon, a purple tail, had chewed through the bars and escaped. It had been an error on Finnius's part, and a costly one. Two lizardmen were dead and one acolyte. High Priestess Selene would have been furious if she knew. Now, the draykis remained on guard as well. They could handle the dragons, but some cleric magic was needed as well.

One acolyte sprinkled the cages with a mix of colorful powder. The dragons snorted and scooted away as he dusted. The elements adhered to the bars, glowing at the sound of the acolytes' words of power and spreading with a dark blue glow up and down the bars. From one cage to the other they went, one sprinkling and the others chanting, until all were finished.

"Very well executed," Finnius said, "and now I have another mission for you."

They bowed.

"Anything, Finnius."

"You, get word to our brethren in Quintuklen. See to it rumor of this temple finds the ears of

Nath Dragon. And you, send word to the High Priestess Selene. Tell her that the trap is set. Go!"

Finnius took a seat on the stone bench and wiped his sweaty palms on his robes. Capturing Nath Dragon wouldn't be easy. He'd seen the man in action before. He eyed the draykis.

"He's faster than you. That sword of his can split an anvil in two."

The lead draykis folded his arms over his chest and said, "Do not underestimate us. We are many; he is one. He may be fast," The draykis flexed the thick scaled cords in his arm, "but we are strong."

"Certainly," Finnius dabbed the sweat from his head with a satin cloth. *They are a cocky lot. But they'll have to do.*

CHAPTER 24

"**B**EN, HAVE YOU EVER SLEPT in a dungeon before?"

"No," Ben said, confused.

"It's the worst food you'll ever eat and the worst company you'll ever keep. But, as they say, 'What doesn't kill you makes you wish you'd died anyway'.

Ben gulped as the soldiers, each brandishing a long spear, approached.

"What's going on here? Are you harassing our citizens?" one said, helping the fallen child up.

Trouble with the local authorities was the last thing I wanted in Quintuklen. They kept things in order, and they had more dungeons here than in all the rest of Nalzambor. I'd been in their dungeons, and they were the last place in the world you'd ever want to go.

"The funny looking one kicked me," the boy said, pointing. "Said he'd kill me if I didn't move."

"Liar!" Ben exclaimed. "I did no such thing. He tried to steal my boots. They all did."

The soldiers weren't much better than children in some cases. They'd rob you blind as well. I could see it in their eyes; they knew Ben was new to the city.

"Where'd you get that armor? It's not a very good fit," one soldier spoke up. "It looks stolen to me."

Ah great. I could see the dungeon doors closing on me now. I hadn't been back in the city five minutes, and I was about to be arrested. I had to do something, fast.

"Soldiers of Quintuklen, may I address?"

They turned and stared.

I leaned forward on my saddle horn and said, "We're just passing through. Supplies for us, food for the horses, one night's rest, and maybe a trip to Dragon Pond out west. My friend's never been to the city, either. He's from the country; can't you tell? But, his uncle..." I eyed Ben.

"Louis of Quinley," he sputtered out.

"Yes, Louis told us to stop in at the Garrison and say hello." I crossed my arms over my chest and shot each man a discerning look.

They glanced at one another, and a moment later the leader said, "Move on!"

"But what about my justice, Soldier?" one of the children said.

"Shaddap, you lazy little rodent, before I whip you." He swatted at one. They scattered. "Troublemakers, the lot of you!"

"Are we really going to the Garrison *and* Dragon Pond?"

"Maybe," I said. Well, now I'd possibly told a lie. I didn't have any plans to take Ben anywhere else with me; I just wanted to get him settled in and go. And with any luck, his Uncle Louis could take him in for a spell.

The farther into the city we went, the less commotion occurred. Quintuklen was well laid out and organized. Gardens, fountains, colorful storefronts and banners could be seen all along the way. The streets were cobbled, and lanterns were lit by magic at every turn of a corner. In the good parts, at least.

"Dragon, can I stay with you one last night? I know you're wanting to get rid of me, and I can only guess you're going to set me up with my uncle," he said atop his horse, dejected.

I felt bad now. I liked having Ben around. He was like a younger brother, and none of my dragon family ever hung around much. Ben had saved my life... and he'd almost gotten me killed. I had things to do.

"Tell you what, Ben. I've got a few things to

do around town, and I guess you can follow if you like. But, I've got business. Serious business. Dangerous, sometimes. You follow my lead. Any more foul ups, I'm leaving you lost in this city."

He shot up in his saddle, showing all of his teeth.

"Thank you!"

"Don't foul up. I mean it!"

He frowned again.

"Come on; let's get inside some walls and have a tasty meal. I guess I'm feeling a little cranky."

Horses clopping over the cobblestones, we made our way down the street. It was dark, but the lanterns made for ample light, but I didn't like that. I liked places that were more discreet. Not where the merchants went, but where the adventurers, soldiers and troublemakers went. They always had the most interesting stories to tell. We stopped in front of a stable.

"This is good," I said.

A young girl came out. She had a button nose and her hair was pulled back in a ponytail. Her eyes lit up when she saw me.

I smiled and flipped her two coins.

"One night, Pretty Thing. A meal bag for each as well."

I slid off my horse, and Ben followed suit.

"Anything you wish, Traveler." She grabbed the reigns and said, "I'll brush them both and check their shoes. Just let me know anything else I can do."

"Thank you," I said, rubbing her head. "That will be fine."

"Yes, thank you, Little Miss," Ben added, reaching out.

She ducked under his hand and moved on, taking a glance or two back at me before she was gone.

"You don't have to do that, Ben."

"Do what?"

"What I do. Just stay close. Look. Learn. Listen, Lilly pad."

His face scrunched up as he said, "Look. Learn. And Listen."

He'll figure it out.

A tavern sign hung nearby, and Ben squinted as he read the words above and said, "Hogfarts?" He grabbed his nose and shook his head.

"They have the worst ale in town, Ben. Let's keep going."

The next sign, another block down, seemed more appealing: The Ettin's Toe. A small crowd of men and women, a hard looking bunch, were full of life on the balcony above.

"This will do," I said, stepping up onto the porch.

Two figures came crashing through the door. A very large, bearded man was entangled with a half-orc: soldiers by the looks of their armor. The man bashed the half-orc in the gut. The half-orc walloped the man in the jaw. As the crowd came out jeering, we went in. Ben was pale when we sat down.

"Relax, Ben. It's best you see the best and worst of what the city offers. And, believe it or not, places like this have the best food to eat." I winked. "Trust me."

Wide-eyed, Ben couldn't help but look around. And I couldn't blame him. There were all sorts of people, which was a big part of what I liked about this town. Small torches lit up all the walls but not the corners. Two men as big as ogres sat at the bar with shoulders bulging up to their necks. A squad of bowmen sat in the middle of the room, joking and jesting of high times. Robed women with dark eyes and painted hands read the palms and heads of others in the room. One woman squealed as she sat on the lap of a man in full plate armor, who was tickling her knee. I smiled. There was nothing more entertaining than people. Especially the human ones.

"What can I get you, Handsome?" the barmaid asked. She was a short buxom woman with blonde curls all over her head. "I recommend the roast and biscuits. We have some chicken and egg soup, too."

"Is it hot?"

She fanned her sweaty neck and winked, saying, "Everything is hot in here."

"Then that will do. Oh, and a small bottle of wine as well, Pretty Thing."

"And a glass milk as well, Pretty Thing," Ben said.

The barmaid cackled like a hyena as she walked away.

"Ben, I don't think they have milk in here."

"But that's all I've ever drunk. Well, that and water."

I rolled my eyes. The two big goons at the bar were eyeing us now, and word was spreading.

"Did somebody order a cow over there?" one of the bowmen shouted our way.

The guffaws followed.

"What, what's he mean by that?"

"Next time, just ask for Honey Brown," I said. Honey Brown was ale, but it wasn't fermented. "It won't get you drunk, and your tongue won't take over your mouth, either."

The barmaid returned with two plates full of steaming food in one hand, a bottle of wine and a pitcher in the other. Setting them down, she said, "Sorry, Young Fella, we're all out of milk, but this should hold you over." She tussled the hair on his head.

"Thank you," I said, placing coins in her hand. "And a room is needed as well."

"I'll fluff your pillows myself, Handsome. My, where did you get eyes like that?" she said.

"From my father."

"Mmmm. Mmmm. Mmmmm. He must be something special as well."

"He is." I looked at our hands. "You can let go now."

"Oh," she blushed, walking away with a swing in her hips.

Ben was stuffing his face full of food.

"I'm starving," he raised the tankard to his lips.

I stopped him.

"Let me see that." I sniffed it. "Honey Brown. You're in good shape. Enjoy."

You couldn't be too careful in a place like this. I'd seen more than one man the night before his first adventure who'd never make it out of the tavern. People would do all sorts of rotten things to one another when you weren't careful.

I sawed up a bite of food and stuffed the meat in my mouth. *Tender and greasy, just how I like it.* And the biscuits, almost more butter than bread, were delicious. I never got to eat things like this in Dragon Home.

"Honey Brown, is it?" Ben said, gulping it down. "Tasty like a thousand honey suckles." He looked over his shoulder. "What are we in a place like this for? What are you looking for?"

"Dragons."

"In here?"

The tavern door slammed open, causing Ben to jump in his chair.

"TORMAC WINS!"

The large man who'd been fighting outside moments earlier sauntered in, dusting off his hands. His beefy forearms were scraped up, and his beard reminded me of an oversized dwarf.

"Does anyone else want to tangle with Tormac?" he said, walking over and slapping the two goons sitting at the bar on the shoulder. "Anyone?"

Heads down, they shook their heads. They were big men, hardy, but not as big as Tormac.

Ben, chewing a mouthful of food, was all eyes as he gawped at Tormac.

"Ben," I said, snapping my finger, "eyes over here!"

He didn't budge.

The crowd fell silent when the leering Tormac said, "What are you looking at, Bug Eyes?"

CHAPTER 25

TURNING PALE, BEN CHEWED ONCE and stopped.

Tormac was a warrior. He had the scars to show for it. The steel on his wide hips was heavy, and the dark eyes over his big flat nose made him all the more menacing. This was not what I needed.

"Well, Bug Eyes?" Tormac said in a grizzly voice, smashing his fist into his hands. "What are you staring at?"

"Don't hurt him, Tormac! He hasn't had his milk yet!" someone shouted.

The tavern erupted in laughter. Ben's cheeks turned red.

Tormac chuckled as he pawed at his beard.

"What's the matter, Bug Eyes? Did you leave your cow at the farm?"

More laughter.

Ben looked at me. Tormac looked at me. All eyes were on me.

I hitched my arm over the back of my chair, leaned back, tossed my hair over my shoulder, and said, "What are you looking at... Ogre Nose?"

It got so quiet I could hear Tormac blink. I continued.

"The last time I saw nostrils that big, dwarves were mining copper out of them."

Somebody laughed, somewhere. I think it was the barmaid.

"What!" Tormac said, hand falling to his blade.

"Ah, good idea. Get your nose picker out. I think I see a boulder... er... I mean a booger in there."

Chuckling ensued. Tormac leered around, bringing the chuckles to an abrupt stop.

"Or is that a toothpick? You could use it; I can see a halfling wedged in that gap between your teeth."

The entire room erupted.

"BRAHHHH—HA-HA-HA-HA!"

My chair clacked on the floor as I teetered forward and stood up, smiling.

Tormac's face was as red as his beard.

"You're going to die," he said through clenched teeth.

I fanned my hand in front of my face and said, "What happened with you and that half-orc out there? Did you eat him?"

149

Food fell from Ben's mouth. The entire tavern was doubled over now, except Tormac.

He swung.

I ducked.

"Let's settle this at the table," I said, dodging another swing. "My arm against yours."

Tormac stopped. An ugly smile started on his face. He was taller than me and as thick as an anvil, an over-sized man with the girth of a dwarf. I was strong. As strong as any man, but Tormac was more than that. He was a mountain. He pulled out a chair and sat down.

To the cry of cheers, I joined him. I looked at my right arm, my dragon arm. It was still well concealed. And Tormac, I'd known he was right handed when he reached for his sword. Of course, you could always tell by which side of the hip it rested on.

We locked hands.

"I win, you leave. You win, I leave." I scanned the crowd. Hope filled the eyes of some. "For good."

"Hah!" He nodded. "You'll be leaving alright," he growled, "in pieces. Your friend, too."

The barkeep raised his arms, hushing the crowd, then wrapped both hands around our knuckles. "That's odd," the barkeep said, looking at me, "you have very rugged skin."

"Get on with it," Tormac said, sneering. "I

broke that last man's arm at the elbow, and I'm going to do worse to yours." He spat juice on the floor.

I winked.

His knuckles turned white as he began squeezing my hand. I'd never arm wrestled such a big, big man.

"Ready," the barkeeper started, "Set... Wrestle."

Tormac put his shoulder into it, shoving my arm down. The crowd roared as my arm bent towards the table. He was strong. Every bit as strong as he looked. A real brute who knew what he was doing.

"Come on, Dragon!" Ben shouted.

I stopped the descent inches from the table and heaved back. Tormac's eyes widened as I began pushing his arm back.

The lively crowd found new life.

"He's pushing Tormac back!"

"Impossible!" someone said.

I loved the attention. I put more dragon muscle into it.

"Hurk!"

I forced Tormac's arm past the starting point and back.

"Golden eyes is winning!"

Sweat dripped from Tormac's forehead and down his nose. The salty taste of my own sweat stung my eyes. I pushed his arm downward little by little.

"NO!" Tormac yelled. "No one beats me!"

The big man snorted in fury, shoving me back, up, up, to the starting point and backward. The entire tavern exploded with shouts of cheers and triumph.

I felt my own ears redden now. My dragon arm was aching. It was fast, but how strong was it, actually?

"Hang on, Dragon!" Ben shouted.

I was, barely. I fought back with everything I had, shoving the brute's arm back. We teetered from the starting point, back and forth. Part of the crowd was chanting...

"Tormac! Tormac! Tormac!"

The other part chanted...

"Dragon! Dragon! Dragon!"

I liked that, but it wasn't helping. Tormac shoved my arm back down, my knuckles barely an inch from the table.

Tormac was huffing and puffing. I held on. Arm throbbing, head aching, I fought on. I didn't care who you were, or what you did, I wasn't going to lose to anyone. Not while I lived. I shoved back with everything I had.

Tormac's eyes were full of triumph as he said, "You're finished!"

Something in the man's face angered me. An evil menace lurked there. A bully. A man of violence. A troublemaker. A thug for hire. A kidnapper. Maybe a murderer. I could see the truth. This man had preyed on the weak all his life. Used his gifts for evil, not good. My inner furnace was stoked.

"No, Tormac," I growled, "You're finished, not I!"

I shoved his arm upward. My dragon arm may not have been stronger, but it hadn't tired.

"No!" Tormac snarled.

Our wrists reached the starting point, and Tormac's arm when down.

The roaring crowd were jumping to their feet!

"Dragon! Dragon! Dragon!"

Tormac was shaking his head. Desperation filled his eyes. I took a quick deep breath and shoved everything into it.

"Nooooooo!" Tormac pleaded.

Wham!

I slammed his knuckles onto the table.

Chest heaving, I managed to say, "Time to go, Tormac!"

The crowd was all smiles as they helped the exhausted man out of his chair. His eyes were weak as he held his arm and was shoved towards the door with the crowd turning on him.

"Get out of here, Tormac! You stink the place up."

"Be a stranger!"

"Your mother's a bugbear!"

Raising my arm in the air and waving, I said,

"That's enough, everyone. It's time to celebrate that he's gone."

The room fell silent.

I had a very bad feeling.

Someone gasped.

Others pointed.

Ben was pointing to his arm.

I looked at mine. My dragon arm had returned. Black as the night. Strong as steel. Beautiful as a black pearl. "Welcome back," I said.

"What manner of trickery is this!"

"He's a changeling!"

"A demon!"

"Fiend!"

I shot Ben a look and mouthed the words, "Get to the horses!"

Something as big as a ham and hard as a rock smacked into my face.

CHAPTER

26

TORMAC LEERED OVER ME WITH a face filled with fury. The man, I hated to admit, punched like an ogre. I could only imagine his booted heel descending towards my head would be twice as bad. Seeing spots, I rolled, gathered my feet, and sprung away. All the people who'd cheered me on moments before now screamed for my head.

"Cheater!"

"Changeling!"

"Kill him!"

"Bash his face in, Tormac!"

My, the tides change fast here.

A wooden tankard zinged past my head.

"Hold on!" I shouted, holding my arms up. "No one stated any rules! I've deceived no one. All I did was make a challenge to arm wrestle. Tormac

Agreed! He lost. I won. Now back away!" I said, shaking my fist.

No one moved. I had a way of capturing people's attention like that.

One woman in the back, dressed in a black vest of leather armor, spoke up.

"Men in disguises can't be trusted! Get him!"

"But—"

The two big goons who sat at the bar seized my arms, locking them behind my back. By the look and smell of them, they were ugly brothers. And not just any type of brothers, but wrestlers, judging by their tattoos and scars and how they locked up my arms.

"Them's scales on his arms," one said.

"Never seen anything like that," said the other. "He's a monster of some sort!"

"A changeling! They're Evil; Burn him!" A woman shouted.

"He's a Demon! No one has gold eyes like that!"

"Hold him still!" Tormac said, rolling the sleeves up on his bulging arms.

"Tormac," I said, "you don't want to do—*oof*!"

The belly blow lifted me off my feet. I groaned.

"That..."

"Hit him once for me, Tormac!"

This can't be happening.

Whop!

I couldn't speak or breathe, and I swore my

156

stomach was screaming from the other side of my back.

"Let's see if we can't take care of that smart mouth of yours."

He swung at me.

I jerked back, letting Tormac's fist hit one of the goons in the face.

"Watch it!" the goon said.

"Don't hit him in the face; he's too handsome!" one lady said, standing on a table wearing a helmet of lit candles on her head.

"Thank you!"

"No, hit him in the face!" one of the bowmen said.

"What is wrong with you people!"

Whop!

Tormac belted me in the stomach again, draining my strength from my head to my toes. I tried to fight, but the goons held me tight. They were like two pythons around my arms.

Whop! Whop!

Tormac laughed. "I told you you'd leave in pieces. *Pow!*

My teeth clattered in my face. *I have no business being here without Brenwar.* I'd settled for Ben the Lilly Pad, instead.

"Get him out of here!"

My body was moving, but not by a will of its own. I could hear the jeers as my knees were dragged across the floor.

"One!"

I felt the wind rushing past my ears.

"Two!"

My stomach was teetering inside my belly.

"Three!"

I was flying.

Crash!

Through a window I went, skipping over the cobblestone road. Struggling, I rolled onto my elbows, groaning when I touched my bleeding lip.

Everyone else spilled out of the doors or were gawping out the broken window.

I waved, saying, "Never let it be said The Ettin's Toe isn't full of charming hospitality."

Someone grabbed me by my shoulders and began pulling me up to my feet.

"Come on, Dragon."

Thankfully, it was Ben.

"Ah look, Bug Eyes has come to help his Demon friend."

"I'm not a Demon!" I said, grabbing my saddle. My leg wobbled in the stirrup as Ben shoved me up into the saddle.

It sounded like the entire city burst into laughter.

"Soldiers!" someone said, pointing.

"Tell them we've found a demon!"

I'd had enough already. I wasn't about to spend the night in jail. Even worse, I didn't need to be accused of being a demon by soldiers.

"Follow me, Ben!" I said, snapping my reigns.

Tormac waved and laughed as we galloped away.

From one side of the city to the other we'd gone when I came to a stop. Tired, aching and weary, I slid from my saddle and took a seat on a stone bench in a long-forgotten park. It was the Garrows. An old part of the city: quiet, discreet, creepy.

"I don't like this place," Ben said, eyes flitting around.

"It's not so bad in the daytime. See," I pointed.

Statues, fountains and gardens were everywhere, but shaded in grey and black, leaving an eerie feeling in the air.

"Come on, I've a friend I was going to check on anyway. Now's as good a time as any," I said, clutching my side.

"You alright?"

"Just a couple of broken ribs," I said through my teeth. They hurt. How many more beatings was I going to take over Ben? Everywhere he was came trouble.

"Sorry, Dragon. I know it's my fault. I should have stayed in the country."

Yes! Yes, you should have!

I didn't say it, however. It was his life. He had the right to do what he wanted. *But I think he'd start to think first more often if his ribs got busted, not mine.*

"This is it," I said, wrapping my reigns around a lantern post.

A single building, no wider than ten feet, stood in stark contrast to the larger buildings at its sides. There were no windows, only an open doorway with stairs leading up.

"You first," I said.

"What about the horses? We can't leave them here."

"Do you see any people?"

He looked around and shook his head.

"No."

"They'll be fine then. Trust me."

Standing at the bottom and looking up, a stairwell lit with small gemstone lights led to a doorway at the top.

"Is that?" Ben squinted, leaning forward, "a door?"

"Yes."

"It looks like it's a hundred yards away, more maybe."

"Then we better get started."

"But?"

I grabbed him by the collar and shoved him forward, saying, "Trust your feet, not your eyes this time."

Up the steps we went. One flight. Two Flights. Three Flights. Ten flights. My body ached with every step. Ben was huffing in front of me, eyes wide as saucers as he kept staring back.

"Keep going."

Twenty flights. Thirty flights. Ben stopped, hands on his knees, scrawny chest heaving, looking back.

"Dragon, what is going on? We aren't going anywhere!"

I cast a look over my shoulder. We were only one flight up from where we started, and I could see the tail of one horse swaying at the bottom.

I smiled. "We're almost there, Ben. Keep going."

Forty Flights.

"You did good back there, Ben."

"I did? How?" he said, wheezing.

I took a breath.

"You got the horses as you were told. You got out of harm's way like I said. If you hadn't, you might be dead, but you'd have been beaten up pretty bad still."

"But you got hurt."

"True, but I'm used to it." I squeezed his shoulder. "Up. We're almost there."

Fifty Flights.

Sweating like orcs, we both let out sighs of relief as we placed our feet on the landing at the top. It was marble, checkered in red and green, with the pattern of a mage on the bottom.

Both of us looked back. We still weren't any farther than when we started.

"I don't understand," Ben said, blinking.

"And you probably never will."

I reached past him and grabbed the ring of a gargoyle faced knocker.

Bang! Bang! Bang!

It echoed like thunder.

Ben stuck his fingers inside his ears.

"Who lives here?" he asked.

"Bay—*ulp*!"

The marble floor disappeared beneath our feet, and into the black we went.

CHAPTER

27

BRENWAR INSPECTED THE HORN HE had strapped around his shoulders. It was a horn carved from bone and gilded with brass and iron. It had two purposes. One was to make noise that was privy to dwarven ears. The other was to listen.

He took the small end and held it in his ear.

From a hilltop, he looked down on a small village. A few hundred residents lived there, and he knew that they, like most small towns, weren't welcoming to dwarves. He could hear voices, talking, and laughter, all of it as clear as a bell. After an hour of listening, he huffed. There were not sounds nor any talk of Nath Dragon. He slung the Dwarven Horn back over his shoulder.

"Two-Hundred years old and he still acts like

a boy." He huffed. "And to think: he might live another thousand years."

Steady through the night he went, down the hill, through the trees. The sun and the rain and the days without sleep did not slow him. His brethren had been scattered towards all of the major cities, seeking for signs, yet none of them had sent word. The Dwarven Horn could send a sound over the air that only the dwarves with other horns could hear. It was dwarven magic, rare and ancient, more pertaining to their craft. One horn linked to another, forming a network of dwarven logic and mystic bounds. Normally, they were used in times of war.

"We should have found him by now," he muttered under his beard.

He knew Nath would be looking for dragons. His friend could be anywhere in the world. But it would be easier to find a needle in a haystack if that's what Nath wanted.

He combed his stubby fingers through his black beard, eyeing it.

"There better not be any pixies in there," he warned. "Hmmm... perhaps my thinking is wrong. Should I be searching for Nath, or searching for dragons?" One would certainly lead to the other. "Perhaps the Clerics of Barnabus?"

What if the clerics had already trapped the man? Nath's father had said, "Keep him from the hands of Barnabus."

Many of the people in Nalzambor thought the clerics protected people from the dragons, unaware it was the other way around. But the clerics were a devious lot. Doing good deeds in the day and dark things in the night. Many were fooled by that, and many were not. Barnabus had been a great warrior who fought alongside the dragons long ago, but now his memory had been turned into something else. No longer a dragon warrior, as the seers said, but a dragon hunter.

Just thinking about it made Brenwar want to pull his beard out.

"If men were as honest as dwarves, we'd never have all these problems."

Miles from the next settlement, he put the horn to his ear and listened hour after hour in the pouring rain.

"Nothing," he grumbled, then traveled on.

CHAPTER

28

"BAAAAAAAAAAAAY-ZOG!" I SCREAMED AS I fell. I couldn't even see Ben, but I could hear him in the darkness.

"HEEEEELP MEEEEEEEE!"

There was light.

Thud!

Pain.

Thud!

And Ben landing on top of me. Whatever hadn't hurt before hurt now, and everything else was worse. I pushed Ben's groaning body off of me and rose to my feet.

The room was filled with brilliant lights, colorful cushions and silk drapes. The incense was so strong I could almost taste it.

"Whew! What is that?" Ben said, fanning his face.

I jerked him up to his feet.

"Just relax, Ben. He'll be offended if you don't."

"Who?" he said, pinching his nose.

Shuffling towards the center of the room, I said, "Bayzog, I know you wish to greet, else I would have landed on a harder floor."

"How big is this place?" Ben said, spinning around. "It was just a tiny building."

It was a huge room, like the ballrooms in the castles. A large sphere of square cut crystals twinkled above. The floor was hardwood, the room a rectangle, with a fireplace of burning logs in every corner. Huge cushions were scattered all over the room, and in the middle was a large square table, waist high and no chairs. Bayzog stood there, staring down into a book the size of ten. He turned and spoke in a strong dark voice.

"If I'd known you were coming, I'd have left a pillow out... maybe." He bowed. "Unwelcome, Nath Dragon."

"Not glad to be here," I replied.

Bayzog was black-haired, small-framed, but sturdy. He wore a red wizard's tunic embroidered with arcane signs and symbols. Everything was impeccable about his character, and his violet eyes were bright, deep, probing. He was part-elven, rich and full of mystery.

I extended my dragon hand.

"My, how eerie are those? He grabbed my arm

and started needling it with his fingers. "Nath, I've never seen black dragon scales before. But I've heard about them."

"You have?"

He grabbed a clear glass lens the size of a fist off of his table and took a closer look.

"Certainly."

"Sorry, of course you have." I said. "What can you tell me about them?"

"Hold on," he said, glancing over Ben. "Hmmm... I see you've replaced Brenwar... obviously a good choice." He grabbed Ben's hand, blinking.

"Nath," Ben said, pulling away, but Bayzog held him fast, "what is he doing?"

"Just be still, Ben. If he wanted to harm you, you'd know already."

Studying Ben though, Bayzog said, "My, this one's nothing but trouble, isn't he?"

"Er... what do you mean? I'm not trouble." Ben looked at me. "Am I?"

I shrugged.

Ben tried to pull away again, but Bayzog closed his eyes and held him fast.

"Hmmm... could be good... could be bad." He released Ben. "He needs more time, Dragon." Opening his eyes, Bayzog said, "And some polishing up will do. Sasha!"

A lovely woman, all human, appeared in white robes.

"Sasha," I said, unable to contain my smile, "It's been too long."

She brushed her auburn locks of hair from her blue eyes and said, "It's good to see you, too, Dragon." She took Ben by the hand and said, "Come along."

Ben, stupefied, said nothing as she led him, smiling, out of the room. I felt like a boulder had rolled off my chest.

"Unthank you, Bayzog."

"Unwelcome, and don't worry; she'll find suitable stitchings, but you'll have to do the rest," Bayzog said.

"I'm not doing anything. I agreed to bring him to the city. Promised him a meal and good rest. He's off to the Legionnaires after this."

"No he isn't," Bayzog said, thumbing through the book's huge pages.

"Yes he is," I objected. "And if you like him so much, he can stay with you."

"Did you come here to argue with me, or did you come for my help?"

I came to get answers. When it came to dragons, Bayzog could deliver. He knew almost as much about dragons as I did.

"Alright, what's in that big book of yours?"

Somehow, Bayzog had everything he ever learned in one book. The Book of Many Pages. It was one big book, or tome rather, on one big table, accompanied with magic ink and quill.

"You know, I have many things in this book. Stories, legends, maps, spells, histories. Everything I've ever learned or heard is right here."

"How do you add more pages?"

His cheerless face brightened a little.

"It can add as many as I need. That's why I made the book."

Looking at it, I said, "That's a lot of pages. How do you know where to look for something? Where do you start?"

"Book, black dragon scales."

The pages came to life, stirring the air, ruffling my hair before they came to a stop.

"Impressive." I squinted. The words would shift and move as I read. I leaned away, pinching the bridge of my nose, and stepped back. "How do you read that? It hurts my eyes."

He showed a wry smile.

"Right. I understand, Wizard. So, what does it say?"

"The color of scales on black dragons," he said, running his finger down the page. "Rare. No black dragons seen since the last dragon war."

He closed the book and stepped away.

"What did you do that for?"

"Nath, tell me what happened. How did you get that arm? You're supposed to get scales, but black ones?"

I'd been friends with Bayzog over a hundred

years, and he knew my story and who my father was. He was fascinated by dragons, but in a good way. So, I told him about the people I killed in Orcen Hold and the last conversation I had with my father.

"But," I showed him the white spot on my hand, "I think I'm turning things around. I even saved a steel dragon and found a Thunderstone."

Bayzog's eyes lit up.

"Do you still have it?"

"No, the steel dragon swallowed it."

Pacing back and forth, Bayzog said, "That's a shame."

"Losing the Thunderstone?"

"Yes to that. No," Bayzog frowned, "to never going home again. I know how that feels."

The brief moment of emptiness in his eyes left me feeling empty again as well.

"So, Dragon, what is your plan?"

"I want to rescue dragons. Many of them at once. That will do it! I know the more I free, the more I can be cured. I know you can help me find them. I need to find a flock of dragons!" I grabbed his shoulder. "You have to help me, Bayzog."

"Ahem."

Sasha, now wearing loose fitting robes, re-entered the room with a pleasant smile on her face.

"Where's Ben?" I asked.

"He's taking a nap," she said, drifting to Bayzog's side.

"A Nap?"

"The young man is tired, Dragon." Her blue eyes flared at me. "And *you* should do the same."

Suddenly, my lids became heavy, and I couldn't fight the yawn.

"Ah Sasha," Bayzog wrapped his arm around her waist and smiled, "always trying to comfort her guests."

Covering my yawn, I fought back and said, "No, not this time, Sasha. Last time, you put me down for two days. I appreciate your concern, but your efforts won't work on me this time. I'm ready."

"Ah Dragon, you know she can't help herself. She knows what's best for you, you know. And you look tired. I've never seen a tired dragon before."

I felt tired. My jaw ached, and my face felt swollen. And with every little movement I felt my cracked ribs inside. *And I remember the last time I took a long nap and what happened when I woke up.*

"Come on, Dragon," Sasha pleaded.

A chair slid across the room and stopped beside me.

Magi didn't get guests very often, so when you came, they expected you to stay awhile.

"I'll sit, but you, Bayzog, need to tell me what you know. I saw that look in your eyes before your book closed."

Sasha looked at him and said, "What is it, Bayzog? You can't keep secrets from our friend."

"Please, Dear," he said. "It's a delicate matter. "

She pulled away, fists dropping to her hips.

"Too delicate for my ears?"

Bayzog's hand recoiled to his chest as he pleaded.

"Certainly not, My Love."

I liked Sasha. She was all about the truth, which was uncommon for a wizard. And as I've said, wizards, magic users, and necromancers could not be trusted. Not even an old friend like Bayzog. When it came to power, they had their weaknesses. Sasha, however, wasn't like that. What she lacked in Bayzog's power, she made up for with integrity.

"Well?" she said, tapping her bare foot on the floor.

Bayzog flittered his fingers and muttered the strangest words.

Where one fireplace blazed in the corner, cushioned chairs and a sofa accompanied it now.

"Shall we?" he said, arm extended to the corner.

I limped over and slumped into the furniture.

"It would have been nice if I'd landed on this sofa, rather than your hard floor."

Sasha readied me a drink from the serving station.

"Coffee, Tea or—"

"Wizard's Water would be fine."

She smiled, saying, "Excellent choice."

She poured a red melon-colored drink in a crystal glass and served us all.

Bayzog hoisted up his glass and said, "To old friends."

"And dead enemies," I added.

I drank. Smooth, bitter and invigorating, I felt my mind and body begin to rest. Tea, Coffee, wine, Ale did little for me, but the wizard's magic elixir did much. It filled me, refreshed me and cleared my senses.

"Ah… I needed that." I clopped my glass on the table and leaned towards Bayzog. "So, tell me what you saw, Wizard."

Sasha leaned his way as well, her beautiful eyes intent on his face.

"Dragon, listen, it's not something that I think is worth mentioning. I can't confirm any of it."

"Bayzog, tell him!"

Bayzog, the epitome of poise, slumped back in his chair, face drawn up with worry.

Sasha gasped, "Bayzog, where are your manners?"

He sighed, one eye open, one on my arm.

"Dragon, your arm, its curse is much worse than suspected."

CHAPTER

29

"How much worse can it be?" I said. "And besides," I showed him the white scales in the palm of my hand, "I think it's getting better."

Sasha took my hand in hers and traced her fingers over it.

"I've never felt live dragon scales before, at least not on a man," she said. "They're beautiful."

That made me feel good. After all, how could something beautiful be bad? I knew I was good.

"Sasha, please, can't you tell he's enough in love with himself already?" He paused, looking at me. "You like it, Dragon. Don't you? The raw power it contains."

I reached over, refilling my glass of Wizard's Water.

"Wouldn't you, Bayzog?"

"Power, yes. Cursed power... no. Listen, have you ever seen a black dragon before?"

I shook my head.

"There's a reason for that," he said, sitting back up in his chair. "They're all dead. They all died in the last dragon war."

"So?" I shrugged. "I'm sure many dragons died off in the last dragon war."

Rising to his feet, Bayzog walked over to the fire, rubbing his hands.

"How much did your father tell you about the Great Dragon War?"

I had to think about that. My father had told me many things, but he never spoke about the dragon wars, and I'd never really given them much thought until now.

"I see," Bayzog continued. "Just so you know, legends say that it was the black dragons that started the Great Dragon War."

I fell back in the sofa, glancing at Sasha's eyes. I could see she was worried.

"And my father killed them?" I asked.

Bayzog shook his head slightly, saying, "We don't know that *he* killed them. Any of the dragons could have killed them. But, they were the cause. They were the solution."

I pulled my arm from Sasha. It was no wonder my father was so furious with me. Black dragon's

176

scales. A reminder of the war. But why did I have them? I was good, after all.

"Bayzog, how come I've never heard of this: the black dragons, the war? You'd think I would have crossed paths with it by now."

"There are legends and histories, some true, some not, in some cases neither, others both."

"That's not really an answer."

"Well, the Great Dragon War might be over, but the evil remains. Much of it is hidden from our eyes, but some of it is right in front of us, mixing the truth with lies."

I took another drink because I was feeling weary again.

"Like the Clerics of Barnabus?" I sighed.

"Do you know the legend of Barnabus, Dragon?" Sasha said.

"Well enough, I suppose."

"Oh, show him, Bayzog. Show him how the story unfolded." She batted her eyes at him. "Please."

He frowned at first and then smiled, saying, "You know I can never tell you no."

She huffed. "You tell me no all the time."

"Only when I study."

She whispered in my ear.

"That's all the time."

He brushed his black hair past the point of his elven ear and said, "I heard that."

Then with a twitch of his fingers, the flames swirled into a sea of color. In the flames, the image of a mighty man appeared, fully armored, carrying a great sword over his shoulder.

"Barnabus," Bayzog said. "One of the few Legionnaires who aided the good dragons in battle."

The image of Barnabus was doused in flames as a dragon appeared from behind.

"I love this part," Sasha said, hugging my arm.

Barnabus turned and ran his sword right through its heart. The flames roared out, and only Barnabus remained. You could see nothing of the man, only his armored metal shell.

"Barnabus, the histories say, killed the last black dragon. It was his bravery and his sword, Stryker, that ended the war. But the Clerics of Barnabus would have Nalzambor believe differently. Under his name, they claim to protect us from all kinds of dragons, claiming they are evil, dangerous. We know better, but most people don't. They fear the dragons. They loathe them. They capture them and sell them from the temples of Barnabus."

"Oh, I hate those clerics!" Sasha said, reddening. "I'd kill them all if you'd let me."

"It's not our fight, Dearest."

I eyed Bayzog, saying, "What's that supposed to mean?"

Holding his hands up, he added, "At least not yet. Dragon, I'm fascinated by you and your kind, but it's the people I protect, not dragons. That's your charge. But," he bowed, "I'll help you with whatever you can do."

I felt that Bayzog was holding back. Wizards always did.

"Tell me where the dragons are?"

"I can't help much there, Dragon. They're hiding. The Clerics have their ears, and they have been as thick as wolves' fur out there. And then you, you of all people, come strolling into this city, knowing full well they've a bounty on you."

I jumped to my feet.

"How did you know that?"

He rolled his eyes.

I threw my arms up.

"Of course! Of course you knew! Alright Bayzog, if you don't want to help, just say so."

I slammed my glass down on the table.

Sasha grabbed me, saying, "Dragon, behave yourself. You know Bayzog means well."

"Does he? Sorry Sasha, but I don't have time for games. I took the risk coming here certain you would help me out. But all you offer is fairy tales and water." I glared at Bayzog. "Let me out of this crazy place." I scoured the room but saw no door.

"Calm yourself, Dragon," Bayzog demanded. "You need rest, and your fresh wounds need to be healed. Have a few hours of peace. I'll see if I can find something, and you can leave when I do."

"Let me out now, Wizard!"

"You're a guest; you can leave whenever you wish. But what about your friend, Ben? Will you abandon him as well?"

I'd forgotten about Ben, but I didn't care. I just wanted out of there.

"Yes. Goodbye, Sasha. I hope you stay well."

She kissed me on the cheek and said, "Be careful."

I shot Bayzog another look, and then I closed my eyes. Remembering how this went, I thought of the front door. I opened my eyes and saw the gargoyle knocker. Behind me, the stairs. Maybe I'd been hasty. Maybe I'd been rude, but I had things to do.

I stomped down the stairs.

"I don't need your help anyway."

"Bayzog! What is wrong with you?" Sasha said. "Dragon is our friend, and he needs us."

He sighed as he took her by the hands and said, "Yes, he does need us, but we cannot help him. Only he can help himself. If he can't ... we'll all need help."

"What do you mean?"

Bayzog strolled over to his massive table and opened his book.

"I read something that I can only assume is true."

Sasha gathered beside him, eyes intent of the pages.

"What does it say? You know I can't read it yet."

He said nothing.

"Bayzog, what does it say!" she demanded.

He cleared his throat.

"The ancient scribes say...

And the black dragons were vanquished, and peace was on Nalzambor until the black dragons returned. So it was. So it has been. A Circle. And the last black dragon shall envelope the world forever.

He closed the book and finished, "... this is much bigger than us. I feel for his father. I feel for the world."

CHAPTER
30

"**B**LASTED WIZARDS!"

I wasn't happy. I wasn't mad, but I wasn't happy. Bayzog hadn't really done anything wrong, other than disappoint me. He was holding something back, something big, something bad—about me; I could feel it in my bones. So I wandered, alone on horseback, through the streets from one side of the city to the other.

"What to do?" I mumbled, drawing a few stares from passersby.

The night wasn't much different than the day in Quintuklen, just darker and quieter. I didn't care for it. I liked watching the people, but tonight, I wanted to be alone. I wanted to sulk. But I knew better. Instead, I headed for the wall, near where we came in.

"Should I go or not?" I said. I hated to leave

empty handed. I came here to find out about the dragons, and I couldn't leave without something.

Above, the moon was full like a brilliant pearl, casting dark shadows in every corner. I had an idea. I just needed to find the Clerics of Barnabus. Like Brenwar would say, "Face the problem axe up and head on!"

The Clerics of Barnabus were the problem. Find them; find the dragons. They'd been looking; I'd been hiding. I decided to take my problem straight to them.

"If I were a cleric, where would I be?" I was gazing up at the moon when it hit me. "The Sanctuary." There were always clerics there.

It was early morning when I arrived at the bubbling fountains just outside The Sanctuary's gates. Within, monuments and statues were covered with dew, and clerics in a colorful variety of robes were milling about. The Clerics of Barnabus were easy to spot, and within seconds I spotted a few tattooed foreheads. My first urge was to gallop over there, snatch one, ride off, and beat the information out of him. But, I donned my cloak and pulled my hood over my head. Leaving my horse, I moved in.

About twenty feet away from them, I took a seat on a bench, head down and listening. There was no loud talking in The Sanctuary, but there was a lot of whispering. And much of it was in a language you couldn't understand. The Clerics had their ancient dialects in which they spoke, but I'd picked up on Barnabus words over the years, sort of. But it was Common I heard.

"We've many to sell. Small ones. Dead or alive, as you will," one Cleric of Barnabus said, speaking to a Cleric in stone-colored robes. I could feel my blood run hot. The Stone Clerics drew their power from the rock, and they weren't noble. According to them, the stone was neither good nor bad, only the one who threw it.

"I've no need of such things."

"Any word on dragons?" the Cleric of Barnabus asked. "We aim to keep the world safe from the menace. Keep them under control we must."

"You can tell those tales to the regular folk, but I know better. Most dragons are as good as you are evil. Be gone with you, I say."

"Pardons and Blessings, Stone Wielder." The Cleric bowed and slowly backed away.

Good for him. I'd have to remember that. The Clerics of Stone were neutral, but they weren't fools. It was good to know.

The Clerics of Barnabus split up, spreading the word about dragons from one group to the other. One of them had the attention of a small group in gold lace with heads hidden under their purple hoods. I didn't recognize the order, but there must have been a hundred different ones in Quintuklen. I got up, stooped down, and picked my way through the people. It was getting crowded.

Ten feet away, back turned, I was leaning on a monument when an odd feeling overcame me. Peering around, I caught the eyes of another cleric of Barnabus who quickly glanced away. They couldn't have seen me, could they? I didn't exactly fit in, but there were all sorts of robed figures and cloaked characters in the Sanctuary. I turned away, took a moment, and glanced back. He was gone.

"We have a Yellow Belly, with pollen breath that turns one to stone," I overheard one cleric say. "Some of the dragon tykes that don't have breath yet, they make fine pets, when broken."

I bunched up my fist and fought the urge to walk over there and punch him in the face. I could barely stand it. *Patience. Look. Listen. Learn.* I might explode first.

"Where do we meet?" the cleric in the purple said.

"Five leagues west, in the Crane's Neck. After the sun sets tomorrow. Gold only."

"Agreed."

That's all I needed to hear. As I turned to head back to my horse, it felt like a bucket of ice water hit me when someone said, "Dragon!"

CHAPTER

31

"**D**ELICIOUS, SIMPLY DIVINE," FINNIUS SAID, wiping his mouth with a cloth napkin.

Good food was hard to come by in the Temple ruins, but the lizardmen were excellent hunters, and the acolytes, when prompted, were decent cooks.

Thumping his fist on his chest, he burped as an acolyte refilled his goblet with wine.

"At least the cellar kept the bottles in order all these centuries, and it would be a shame for it all to go to waste, wouldn't it?" he said, eyeing the cage that sat on the small table.

The pixlyn woman was there: tiny, pink, knees drawn up, head down.

"Oh, you can speak to me, little faerie. As a matter of fact, I'd like to hear you sing. They say the song of the faeries is a beautiful and magical thing, but I've never heard it."

Finnius pulled the cage closer and peered in.

"What do you say?"

She didn't budge.

He slammed his fist on the table.

"SING!"

She flinched, then rubbed her tiny fists in her eyes, sniffling.

"Oh, how adorable." He tapped the cage. "Little Pixlyn, sing for me, else I'll pluck your husband's wings off when he arrives."

Her bee wings buzzed as she hovered up, nodding her head.

"Oh, I have your attention now, don't I? Sing, Little One. I want to feel the mystic words you hold. Sing to me," he beckoned, "share your powers... or die."

Her tiny little mouth opened up, and beautiful words flowed out. Not words men could recognize, but a beautiful, ancient language. Harmonious and Delightful.

Finnius sat back and sighed, letting the music fill him from head to toe.

"Wonderful," he muttered. He'd been weary, but no more. His once spent energies from his mission now recharged. His mind refreshed and cleared.

"Excellent," he muttered, slumping back, tears forming in his eyes. *So pure, so good, so amazing.* It was nothing like he'd felt before.

Something banged into the pixlyn cage.

Finnius lurched up, rubbing his watery eyes.

"What?"

The male pixlyn was back.

Finnius shook his head, saying, "What is the meaning of this, Pixlyn?"

The little man's tiny mouth was a buzz of words.

"I see. Hmm... Excellent, I see. Nath Dragon is on his way already." He clapped his hands together. "My, won't the High Priestess be pleased. Tell me. Tell me about it all."

Finnius muttered a spell and sprinkled powder over the pixlyn.

The words of the pixlyn were high and garbled momentarily, and then a sound of man came forth.

"It took me no time to find the man. I told your men who he was and where to go. Your men spread word as I watched. The man overheard the conversation about the dragons. Your men spoke to your men in disguise. The man you want believed it. He and them travel this way now."

"Hah!" He slapped his knee. "Keep me posted then, Pixlyn! Go! Spy!"

The tiny winged man flew into his face and said, "My mate?"

"Yes, well, she'll be quite alright," Finnius flashed a wicked smile, "assuming she keeps her wings, assuming you do as you are told and I don't have to clip her wings. Now go!"

CHAPTER

32

BRENWAR'S STOMACH GROWLED. HE COULDN'T remember the last time he was so hungry. His horse bent its neck towards the stream water and began to drink. His stomach growled again.

"Ah, be quiet, will you?" he said, reaching into his pack and withdrawing peppers and bread. He took a bite. "That might hold you, until we find Dragon, that is."

He hadn't eaten since he left, or slept either. He rubbed his mount's neck, watching the trout swimming upstream. He'd like to fish, but he didn't have time.

"It's a shame you horses don't eat fish," he said. "You don't know what you're missing."

The horse nickered, raising its neck. Brenwar got a sour apple from his saddle bag and fed the horse. At some point, the horse would need rest; he knew. And stopping in the next village might be in order.

"I hate stopping," he grumbled.

"Me too," a deep voice responded from the nearby trees.

Brenwar jumped from his horse and rolled over the ground, rising up with his war hammer ready.

"Who said that?"

The woods were tall, green and quiet. Only the wind and rippling waters hit his ears.

"Easy, Dwarf," a tall figure said, stepping from behind the trees. "Remember me?"

Brenwar squinted his eyes beneath his bushy black brows.

"Bah! You're one of those fat bellied elves."

"And you're one of those short-legged orcs," the Wilder Elf replied.

"I see you've got a death wish, don't ya?" Brenwar said, pointing his weapon. "Come then, I'll make a fine grave for you!"

Eyes twinkling in the light, Shum laughed, like a man laughs at a child. With the grace of the elves and girth of a large man, he approached, swords silent on his hips. He clasped his hands over his belly and said, "I mean you no harm, Dwarf."

"That may well be, but I can't say the same."

Brenwar moved in, taking a chop at Shum of the Roaming Rangers' legs.

The elf sprang away.

"Stop!" Shum held out his arms. "I'm not here to fight, as much as I'd like to teach you a lesson."

"A lesson!" Brenwar rushed.

Shum jumped back, Brenwar's axe clipping his cloak.

Brenwar would fight anyone, any place, any time. Especially an elf. They bothered him. Not so much as orcs and giants, but still, they were elves. Dwarves and elves: both on the side of good, but unable to get along since the days their races were young.

"You would strike me down when I'm not even defending myself," Shum said, aghast.

Brenwar swung.

Shum dived.

"I would."

He chopped.

Shum rolled.

Brenwar kept coming, swinging, chopping.

Shum was off balance as he waded into the waters.

"Stop it, Dwarf! I apologize," he said, holding his arms out.

Brenwar swung his war-axe into water-laden log where Shum's toe had been.

"For what!"

"Calling you a 'short-legged' orc?"

Brenwar stopped and pointed at him.

"No one calls a dwarf an orc and lives."

"Well, you shouldn't call me a fat bellied elf."

Brenwar's black eyebrows cocked over his eyes.

"But you *are* a fat-bellied elf."

Shum huffed, dragging himself out of the water, towering over Brenwar, and replied, "And proud of it." He extended his arm. "Can you talk, Brenwar?"

They bumped forearms, outside, then inside.

"Aye," Brenwar said, "what is it you want?"

"Nath Dragon."

Brenwar walked over to his horse and fed it another apple.

"Why?"

Shum's jaw tightened.

"I think we need his help finding our King again."

Brenwar pulled himself up onto his horse.

"I don't know where he is."

"But you're looking for him; I know. I've been following you since you left Morgdon. I was waiting for him, but he never came, only you. I've been trying to figure out what was going on, but I didn't realize you'd lost him until now."

Brenwar stiffened in his saddle, saying, "What do you mean, days? I got attacked by brigands, and you didn't help!"

"And you handled them quite well. I respect your skills, Brenwar, and I'd have aided if needed."

"Humph! What makes you think Dragon can

help you find your king? You're the best trackers in the land, aren't you? Why would you need Nath?"

Shum ran his long finger back and forth on his chin and said, "It's just a theory really, but we think they are linked. They have the same needs."

"Pah," Brenwar started leading his horse away. "They aren't linked. He's an elf or an ape, and Dragon is a man, or a dragon. He shall tend to his affairs, the dragons; you attend to yours, the elves or... er the apes."

"We're all linked whether we admit it or not. Dragon has a curse. My King is cursed. It's a common evil they share."

"It's your king, not mine, not his. And, Nath is not evil, and I can't say the same for your king." Brenwar waved as he galloped off. "Goodbye, Fat Bellied Elf!"

Shum shook his head, watching him go as he said, "I can walk faster than that little horse can run." He took off at a trot. "You're getting my help whether you want it or not, Dwarf. Too many lives depend on it."

Chapter 33

"**D**RAGON!"

I whirled, knocking a man over. It was Ben. Despite the bewildered look on his face, I could have killed him.

"What are you doing here?" I exclaimed under my breath, lifting him up and with haste guiding him away.

"Bayzog—"

"Keep it down, you idiot," I hissed through my teeth.

Every eye in the sanctuary was looking.

"Sorry, Drag—"

I squeezed his arm.

"Quiet, will you?"

"Ow," he whined as I dragged him to where my horse was, as discreetly as I could.

His horse was next to mine.

"How did you do that?" I said, grabbing the reigns and getting out of The Sanctuary.

"Bayzog did it, how I don't know. I was talking to him, and he said you'd be here, and I said, 'Where?' and poof, here I was. He said you needed to come back, that he had some information for you that could help." He rubbed the back of his head. "Sorry, Dragon, did I do wrong again?"

"Get on your horse," I ordered.

I was angry. If Ben had shown up seconds earlier, it could have ruined everything, and I wasn't so sure it hadn't. When I glanced back, all the bald heads and purple robes were gone.

"Great."

I led; Ben followed.

"Are we going back to Bayzog's?"

"No."

"He said you'd say that, but he also said, um..." he looked up into the sky, "It's your burial, not mine."

"Figures." *Lousy wizard!* "Listen Ben, you didn't do wrong, but you aren't coming along, either. I'm taking you to the Legionnaires to be with your uncle."

Ben shook his head.

"No! I don't want to go. Please, I want to stay with you! I'm ready, see?" He pulled his cloak open, revealing a well-fitted tunic of leather armor. A nice sword and dagger were belted at his sides. I could tell by the pommels they were elven made. He even had boots to go with it.

"So, you think if you get some armor that fits and sharp and shiny blades that makes you a soldier? You haven't even had any training, Ben. You almost died once on the way up here, and now I'm heading into the mouth of danger. You think you're ready for that? Do you?"

Biting his lip, he fingered the pommel on his sword.

"We'll just go back and see what Bayzog says. It was important."

"No, Ben. I'm on my own from here. Now don't follow me anymore."

Good luck or bad luck Ben was, according to Bayzog. The part-elven wizard had a way of reading people.

"Bayzog said I should come, no matter what."

I stopped my mount.

"Really Ben, how well do you know Bayzog? You barely spent a minute with him in there."

"Well, it's not him so much as," he smiled, "Sasha. Ooh … She is so beautiful."

"And troublesome, Ben." I got closer and checked his blades. "Fine steel for a wizard to keep. What else did they give you?" I reached into his belt pouch. Two potion vials were within. "What do these do?"

"He said I'd know when to take them."

I slapped Ben upside the head.

"Ow!"

"You don't know when to do anything!"

I'd had enough and headed for the wall. It was time to make way for the Crane's Neck, and I didn't care whether or not Ben followed.

"So be it, Ben. It's only your life."

The trip was long. Not because it was far, but because my tongue was tired from trying to convince Ben not to go. He wouldn't have any part of it, however.

"It's my life; I'll do what I want with it," he'd decided, saying it over and over, with his chin up.

Oddly, he was starting to remind me of Brenwar—aside from his shivering in the rain.

The Crane's Neck wasn't hard to find. It was a valley of enormous rocks, some of which looked to be left over from a battle between the giants. I followed a faint trail over the brush and climbed up a rocky cleft that overlooked the Crane's Neck. It was a rock, stretching fifty feet in height, shaped like a long flowing neck. The setting sun peeked from behind the dark clouds, shining on the beak-like peak at the top.

"Lie down. Be quiet. Don't move." I said to Ben, lying down myself.

Ben did. I actually wanted to thank him. It wasn't very often that he did what I said.

"It'll be a few hours before dusk, so we'll just lie low for now. Got anything to eat?"

Ben shook his head.

"Great. I'm surprised Bayzog didn't prepare you better. Are you sure one of those vials isn't a bottle of Tasty Wonders?"

He scrunched up his face, shook his head and said, "I don't think so."

"Well, that's too bad. Those are pretty good, and they can hold you over for days. Stupid wizard. You'd think he'd have better prepared you." I looked at him. "Right?"

He nodded, his eyes focused on the Crane's Neck, lying on his belly sopping wet. The rain would start and stop, between drizzle and heavy drops. He shivered, even though it wasn't that cold. At least he was quiet. At least he obeyed for once, and that was a comforting thought.

Rain pelting my face, I sat alongside him thinking. How many dragons did the clerics have? They'd spoken of at least three, but there could be more. I rubbed my dragon arm, imagining if my scales might turn white after I freed them. I could go home then. I wanted to see my father more now than ever, and I couldn't remember ever wanting to see his giant dragon's head so much before. I pulled my hood over my head, sat down, and waited.

A few paths led past the Crane's Neck, some narrow and some wide, between the rocks and ridges. There wasn't much else in the valley, either, just a small variety of trees and bushes, enough to be hospitable to the critters. Another hour had passed when I heard Ben's stomach growl.

"Still glad you came?"

He didn't say anything.

It was getting annoying.

"Alright Ben, you've made your point: you can be quiet."

He rolled over and smiled, saying, "See, I told you I could be a good soldier."

"Indeed," I said, rolling my eyes. "Well, there's no sense in having your ravenous stomach give us away. It could wake up a drunk bugbear. Run down to the horses and fetch the rations hanging from my saddle."

He quickly ambled over the rocks, down and out of sight. I had to admit: I was hungry, too. I rubbed my ribs. Tormac had given me a good walloping, and my jaw still felt loose. It was a shame; he'd be a good ally if he wasn't such a bad man. The world was full of men like him, but there was always something worse. The orcs. The ogres. The goblins. The bugbears and gnolls. You'd think men would act better than them, but often—too many times—they disappointed me. Their short lives made them particularly greedy.

Ben shuffled back over the rocks and fell to his knees.

"Here you go, Dragon," he said, holding out a small sack.

"Eat, Ben."

He reached in the bag and dug in. I grabbed a bite as well.

Ben shook a canteen in my face.

I took it and drank, handed it back, and said, "Drink, that dwarven bread is hard to get down sometimes."

"Kind of bitter," he said, talking a swallow. "But I feel full already."

"Brenwar would kill me if he knew what I was doing."

"Who?" Ben said, looking up at me.

"Oh, sorry Ben, just a friend of mine, a dwarf. He's usually with me on days like this, telling me what I can and cannot do. Or what I should, or should not do."

"Kind of like you do me, huh?"

I felt like I'd swallowed a bug. I was nothing like Brenwar.

"Just eat."

Down in the valley, about an hour later, I noticed a small group of figures coming from behind the Crane's Nest.

"Get down, Ben!"

From our bellies, we could see the Clerics of

Barnabus, five of them in all, and a small cage. I had a pretty good idea who was in that cage, too. A dragon. Two broader figures emerged with spears and armor. Lizardmen. I could feel Ben tense up at my side.

"It'll be alright. Don't move, Ben. Don't make a sound."

The five Clerics faced the path leading from the east. The lizardmen began searching the nooks and crevices in the area. The rain became a steady pour, and I lost sight of the lizardmen.

"Not good, Ben. Not good."

CHAPTER
34

INSTINCT. SOMETIMES IT WAS THE only explanation as to why some men lived while others died. My own had bailed me out many times, but I wasn't sure about Ben as he kept looking over at me. It takes time to develop instincts in some; others it's quite natural. Some don't get it at all.

Keeping my voice low, I said, "What are you thinking?"

"There's probably more of them, isn't there?"

"Good." I was reassured. He wasn't stupid; he had some savvy to him. "Maybe a couple, just keep an eye out."

I rose up to my knee and readied Akron.

Snap. Clatch. Snap.

"You going to shoot them?" Ben asked.

"Hopefully at some point in time, but right now I'm just being prepared."

"Oh."

I wasn't really sure why I readied my bow. I just did. Something bothered me. Tired, swollen, and stubborn, I felt a little off, and there was a nagging warning bell behind my eyes. Peering through the rain, I looked for any sign, anything odd.

"Can they smell us?" Ben asked.

It was a good question. *Good for him.*

"They're pretty good trackers, but not like most hunters, and their snouts are so, so. It's the orcs you have to watch out for. But, this rain keeps our scent down, plus we're downwind. So, I'd say we're safe for now."

The farther the sun dipped, the colder it seemed as we waited. The lizardmen reappeared about an hour later and gathered near the clerics.

"Dragon, I see something coming," Ben pointed.

I could barely make out the purple through all the rain, but it was the clerics from Quintuklen, riding on horseback.

My heart raced as they greeted one another and revealed the covered cage.

"What is it?" Ben asked.

Despite the heavy rain, I could make out a small white dragon inside. Not just any white dragon, but a long-tailed white. They weren't very big dragons either, but one of the smaller breeds.

"A dragon. A powerful one at that."

Below, I could see no coins were exchanged,

and the talk had stopped. The Clerics of Barnabus led, and The Clerics from Quintuklen followed.

"Are we going to rescue it?"

"Don't you worry about that," I said, grabbing his shoulders. "Now listen to me Ben, and listen good."

He was all ears.

"Stay with the horses. There's plenty of food with them. If I'm not back in two days, go back to Quintuklen and see Bayzog and Sasha. Just tell them what you know, not that it will matter."

"But, I want to go."

I squeezed his shoulders until he grimaced.

"I'm counting on you. We can't follow those men on the horses. They'll catch us. We can't leave the horses now either, can we?"

He shook his head, eyes down saying, "No."

"What you are doing might not seem important, Ben, but it is. It is to me and to the horses. This is what a good soldier does."

He frowned, saying, "But Bayzog gave me these weapons, and potions too." He unsheathed his dagger and stuck it in my face. "See?"

In a single motion, I twisted it away and jammed it back in his sheath.

"Yes, Ben. Perfect weapons and potions to protect yourself and the horses with." I slapped him on the shoulder. "Remember what I said, and take care, Ben."

As he started to object, I turned and leapt off the ridge, hopping down from one boulder to the other like a Mountain Cat. When I made it to the bottom, I looked up and waved.

He was gaping.

"Sorry Ben, I can't have you following me, now can I?"

Off into the rain I went. I had monsters to stop and dragons to save.

The sun had set by the time I traveled the first league, and the trail was already faint. Ahead, I could see one lizardman had drifted back, waiting. It was a common tactic.

The lizardmen made good guards and soldiers, ferocious soldiers, but not as loyal as hounds. They were known to take bribes now and again. No, the lizardmen were the orcs of reptiles, a blasphemous creation and insult to dragonkind, in my opinion.

I crouched into the bushes, waiting. "Come on," I said to myself, "get going, will you?"

He stood like a statue alongside the path, a dark statue. Five minutes passed, then ten, then twenty.

I heard him chew on something, swallow, spit, then begin to tread up the path.

Finally!

I had followed him another league when he

stopped and waited again. Ahead, I could see a series of hills forming into the perfect place to hide in. "There are always secrets in the hills," the seers said. I hunkered down. *What to do?*

The lizardman was making sure no one followed. But how did I know he was following them, and not leading me somewhere else? With the time all his breaks took, they could have gone anywhere by now. The heavy rain would easily wash away their tracks.

"Drat!" I cursed under my breath.

Maybe they knew I was onto them already.

Frustrated, I ambled down the path.

Twenty paces away, the lizardman stepped full into the path, spear lowered.

I unleashed Akron's arrow into his scaly green thigh.

Thwack!

The lizardman pitched forward, hitting the ground with a painful hiss.

Lizard men don't scream, but they hiss something awful when you shoot them in the leg.

It took a stab at me as I walked over. I sidestepped, then ripped the spear from its hand and broke that over its head.

"I can't have you following me now, can I?"

I slugged it in the jaw, and its eyes rolled up in its head.

"I hope they weren't expecting you. You'll be

awfully late with that arrow in your leg," I said. *Got to move, Dragon.* I didn't have much patience left, and the disturbing thought of caged dragons infuriated me. I hooked Akron on my back and jogged up the path. *It shouldn't be that hard to catch up with a bunch of clerics, even if they do know the terrain better than I.* An hour later, I stopped and kneeled down. I ran my fingers over some muddy footprints in the path. *Excellent!* Through the slop, I forged ahead.

Two more leagues I had followed the trail when the rain let up. The bright stars peeked over the trees, and the waters rushed over the hillside while I heard the sound of people shuffling up ahead. I crept up until I could see them. It was them, a small band of clerics accompanied by one lizardman that guarded the rear.

The path winded up the hill, through the trees and alongside a gulch. That's when I got my first look at it. A temple jutted out in stark contrast to the woods. The exterior wall was overgrown in vines and withered with decay, and many of the stone columns behind it had fallen. The party of men filed through a gap in the wall and disappeared from sight. The lizardman hung back at the gate. I remained behind the trees.

Great.

The temple wall, or what was left of it, was a hundred feet long and fifteen feet high. It ran from hillside to hillside. On the wall, a few lizardmen stood watch, and for all I knew, the place was full of them. Now, I could handle a few lizardmen, but ten or twenty? That would be something.

What to do, Dragon? What to do? Sneak inside, or bust them all in the face?

I unhitched Akron.

Snap. Clatch. Snap.

The string coiled into place.

Clerics. Lizardmen, whoever else. No one was going anywhere until I freed those dragons. I had them trapped.

I whipped out an arrow and rubbed spit on its tip. It twinkled with life. My dragon heart began to thunder inside my chest. I knew the dragons were in there, but not for long. The time to fight had come.

"Show evil no mercy," I said through gritted teeth.

I took a deep breath, nocked the arrow, pulled back, aimed, and let it fly.

Chapter 35

THE ARROW SAILED TRUE TO its mark, smacking into the temple.

KA-BOOM!

My blood coursed through my veins with new energy. Explosive action. That's what I liked. The lizardmen on top went flying up in the air with a shower of rock before crashing to the ground. I don't know if that killed them, but it wouldn't hurt my feelings if it did.

The lizardman at the gate stood gaping at the hole in the temple wall, waiting, uncertain.

Still hidden from sight, I nocked another arrow, waiting. *One. Two. Three...*

Lizardmen poured from the gate, and even more of the reptilian heads popped up over the wall again. *I knew it!* I let another arrow fly. It juttered at the feet of the lizardman at the gate, drawing grunts and cries. I stepped into the clear and waved at them as they raised their weapons at me.

"Wait for it, Snake-Face!" I yelled.

KA-BOOM!

A half-dozen lizardmen filled the sky with green.

A crossbow bolt zinged past my head. Nocking another arrow, I charged the gate. Three reptilian faces peeked over the wall, crossbows pointed at my chest. The crossbows rocked into action as I tried to dodge. A bolt skipped off my chest plate as I let the other arrow fly.

KA-BOOM!

Shards of rock flew everywhere. The top of the wall where the lizardmen stood was a smoking ruin as I scrambled over the rubble and through the smoky hole. I heard the lizardmen hissing and moaning nearby. I put a normal arrow in my teeth and loaded another in my bow. I aimed through the dust and smoke.

Twang!

I caught one in the thigh.

Twang!

Another in the shoulder.

Their loud hisses caused another alarm. I let my other senses guide me through the ruins and dust as another throng of lizardmen came on. I didn't care.

Twang! Twang! Twang! Twang! Twang!
I had plenty of arrows.
Twang! Twang! Twang!
Hisses and smoke were all I heard, and the lizardmen weren't going anywhere without severe limps.

Locating one, I kicked the crossbow out of its hands, wrapped my dragon arm around its neck, and squeezed.

"Where are the dragons?"

Lizardmen could speak; they just didn't speak much.

It shook its head, hissing.

I cranked up the pressure.

"Where are the dragons?"

He pointed his scaly finger as he choked out the word, "There."

Two columns led the way from the courtyard into a narrow tunnel.

"How many more?" I demanded.

"Many clerics. No more Lizard—", it started as a shadow fell over me.

I jerked away.

Clonk!

Something clipped the back of my head, drawing spots in my eyes. It was a lizardman, a big one with brawny arms and shoulders. It reminded me of Tormac, but with scales and not as ugly.

It swung its club into my shoulder, almost breaking my arm as I dove to the ground.

I rolled onto my back, pushed off, and landed on my feet, ripping Fang from his sheath.

Shing!

The bullish lizardman charged, club high, swinging down.

Fang sheared its club in two.

The slits inside the lizardman's skull widened as it stared at what was left of its club. Shielding its eyes from Fang's glow, it backed away.

"Run," I said. "Or die," I warned. "It matters not to me."

Tongue flicking from its mouth, it eyed me and my sword.

Poised to strike, I took another step forward.

It turned, ran towards the gate, and was gone, leaving me alone with a bunch of groaning lizards.

It took everything I had not to kill that big lizardman, and if he had attacked, I'm not so sure I could have held back. I'd had enough of clerics, lizardmen, dragon poachers, orcs ... the whole lot of them.

"You should follow your comrade if you know what's good for you," I said as I headed for the entrance, waggling my sword under the nose of one lizardman as I passed. "You better not be here when I come back, or I'll slice every bit of Lizard from your skin."

Hissing and crawling, they slowly made their way towards what was left of the entrance.

"Good."

Still, my anger rose as I made my way inside the tunnel. I told myself it was the heat of battle, but I loved to battle. I just had to exercise control.

"Just free the dragons, Nath," I said to myself. "Knock all the clerics out if you have to."

Into the darkness I went, following a stone corridor where no torches were lit. My keen eyes could barely make out the faint lines of the corridor I traveled, but I could smell them. The men, the sweat, the evil, and something else.

"Hmmm... Be ready, Fang," I whispered.

His razor-sharp edge hummed in reply, flaring once then winking out.

The air was still: quiet, like a tomb of the dead. Using caution, I planted one foot after the other until I found myself at a crossroads. Three tunnels opened like mouths. There was no telling how far this temple went back into the mountain.

"What do you think, Fang?"

The cold steel didn't sing.

"Thanks." Peering down the middle tunnel, I inhaled. Decay, men, incense and dragons. If I got close enough, I could smell their blood. "A little light would be nice. Besides, I'm sure they know I'm coming—unless of course they are deaf acolytes."

Fang's hum added a soft white light.

"Thanks," I said, making my way down the

213

middle tunnel. That's what Brenwar would have done, I figured. "Take the direct approach," I said in my best Brenwar voice.

Ancient markings—carvings and paintings long worn and faded—lined the walls. It was hard to tell what race of people lived here so long ago because it was another ancient language I did not recognize. A door greeted me at the end, or at least what was left of one. I heard something on the other side and pressed my ear along the door. Beautiful humming or singing grabbed me by the ears and pulled me through.

It was wonderful, sweet, and melodious as a waterfall of honey, removing all the anger and pain from my body. Fearless and care free, I went forward, a smile stretching across my face, ignoring Fang throbbing in my hand.

"It's alright, Friend," I said, sliding him into his sheath.

Drunk with elation, I hummed and twirled my way down the ancient corridor, its pictures and traces now colorful, vibrant and real. I hadn't felt this way in years. I laughed, a hundred laughs in one, following the music.

"Oh dragons," I half sang, half said, "Where are you, little dragons? Come and play with your brother. You cannot hide from me."

The warm glow of a fire was in the distance, and my compulsion drove me onward. Up there must be the most wonderful place in all of Nalzambor. *The dragons*, I thought as I drifted forward, *they aren't prisoners at all, but instead the luckiest dragons in the world*. And somewhere they were being sung to by the most beautiful woman in the world. I couldn't wait to see her as I passed from one room to the other. There she was, simply captivating.

"My, you are so beautiful."

CHAPTER
36

SHE WAS EVERYTHING I IMAGINED. The kind of woman so magnificent, the entire room lights up in her glory. And it did. Fires burned with vibrant life, and many robed men sang praises to her along the walls. Every face was happy, joyous, elated, and my heart cried out in my chest as I longed to be with her. To hold her. To kiss her. To love her like no other.

"Who are you?" I said, stretching out my hands.

Her face was gorgeous: part-human, part-elf, part-dragon, a combination of all the most beautiful faces I'd ever seen.

"Relax, Nath Dragon. Sing." She poured me a goblet of wine. "Drink. You look thirsty."

I took it as her hands caressed my face, and she unbuckled my sword belt and tossed it aside. I didn't even notice the singing acolyte lifting my quiver and bow from my shoulder. No, I was too infatuated with her dark gossamer robes blended in with her lustrous hair and how her toes did not show as she floated over.

"We've been expecting you," she said, draping her long sensuous arm over my shoulder. "Come, sit, rest." She led me towards a magnificent chair and sat me down. "Comfortable?"

My tongue clove to the roof of my mouth, and my mind swirled. I wanted to be with her so bad. I'd do anything she said. But why, the recesses of my mind asked, did she smell so bad? I had to ask.

"You are so amazing, but why do you smell... er... smell so funny?"

Her beautiful face suddenly turned dark as the music stopped.

I shook my head saying, "What's happening?"
Whop!

A fist made of dragon scales lashed out, striking me in the chest. She howled in triumph, her face contorting with rage as she struck again.
Whop!

My neck snapped back, slamming me into the chair.

"What in Nalzambor are you?" I said, holding my busted face.

She growled. Part-animal. Part Something Else.

All the colorful images began to fade, the beauty of the ancient sanctuary melting away, leaving only the fires (which were just torches) and the clerics (some bald as eagles, the others draped like purple curtains).

Behind me, the chair came to life, arms as strong as iron wrapping around me, crushing me.

My dream had become a nightmare, and it was just beginning.

The woman changed as well, her lustrous face and figure drifting like smoke and forming something else. A horrible, hulking abomination loomed over me, almost seven feet of meat, muscles and bone. It was built like a man, and armored, with a face like a dragon and scales, too.

It curled up its clawed hand as big as my face, drew back, and punched me again.

I groaned in pain. I'd thought it was over with the lizardmen.

A human voice cackled as whatever it was that held me slammed me into the ground. I couldn't move. I couldn't breathe. I could feel though. I felt like a pane of glass catching a giant stone.

"Ugh..."

"Welcome to your party, Nath Dragon. I hope you like your surprise," said a robed man with a slight limp in his step.

I looked up, face bleeding, getting a glimpse of the source of the familiar voice through my swelling eye.

"You, I know you," I managed. It was the Cleric

from Narnum, the one who ratted out the Orcen Hold, where the Blazed ruffie was freed. The one I saw the day before my arm turned black. I tried to smile. "Tell you what: if you let the dragons free, I'll go easy on you. It won't be nearly as easy walking with two limps instead of one."

Finnius nodded at his dragonian goons.

One kicked me in the ribs, then the other wrapped his monstrous arm around my neck.

"Easy, Draykis, we need something left of him before dinner." Finnius squatted down beside me. "Tsk. Tsk. Catching you was so much easier than I'd thought it would be, Nath Dragon. Look around. The best plan is a well-executed one. See?" He motioned to the clerics in purple behind him. They pulled back their hoods, revealing the same bald heads with tattooed signs that I had seen in the garden.

I felt like a fool. They'd known I was coming all along. *Ben!*

"Oh, what is wrong, Nath?"

"It's Lord Dragon to you," I said, shifting his focus. Maybe he didn't know about Ben.

He shoved my face into the dirty floor saying, "Fool!"

"Don't touch my hair, you little worm," I warned. "Ow!" I felt a dragon claw poking into my leg. "What are these things... uh... what is your lowly name anyway? Ow!"

He rose, wrapping his hands behind his back, and said, "Finnius. Hah. And even you should know that it only takes a little worm to catch a big fish. A big bald fish once this day is over." Some of the acolytes chuckled as he paced the sanctuary. "Perhaps some of the draykis would be more appealing with some of your locks attached. Or maybe I can fetch a fine price for your hair in the cities."

"It would certainly do wonders for that bald head of yours, but these," I stared over my shoulder, "Draykis are well past ugly. I don't think hair would help. What in Nalzambor are they?"

"Men fused with dragon skin, dragon blood and magic," he said, stepping on my dragon hand. "A glimpse into your future." Looking at my hand under his boot, he went on. "My, what have we here? It seems there is part draykis in you. This is a fortunate day for you indeed, the day you get to see what you are about to become. Dragon? Draykis? Or one and the same."

My stomach knotted. What he said didn't so much anger me as worry me. But, there was a ring of truth to it. I was a man with dragon blood and magic, and there was no telling what I might become.

"So, Finnius the Worm, now that you have me, what is in store for me? Death? Collect a bounty? Sell me off with the other dragons?"

"Oh Nath, as much as the Clerics of Barnabus despise you and your heroic doings, we have no intention of killing you. You see, I follow orders whether I like them or not. It's why I have this limp." He tapped his thigh. "These signs." He fingered the patterns on his head. "And more to command. More power. Why, I even control these powerful draykis." He grabbed a torch off the wall and held it to the standing draykis's mouth. "Eat."

The draykis snatched the torch from his hand and stuffed it inside its mouth, chomping it to splinters and swallowing it whole. It burped a puff of smoke.

"Charming." I struggled to get out. "Show me some more tricks. Can it eat worms, too?"

Finnius bent over, picked up my sword belt and scabbard, and handed it to one of the acolytes. He tossed another one my bow and quiver.

"Take these away," he said.

The bald men disappeared through the door that I came in.

Finnius clapped his hands together. "Now the festivities shall begin."

"You mean ole torch eater has more tricks?"

A wry smile formed on Finnius's face, sending a chill down through my bones.

"I'm not supposed to kill you, Nath Dragon, but the High Priestess didn't tell me how alive she needed you, either."

Finnius almost pinched his fingers together when he said, "Almost dead will do." He waved his arms over his head. "Algorzalahn!"

Finnius disappeared in a puff of smoke, leaving me sealed in the room with the draykis.

"This is going to hurt, Nath Dragon," one said, tugging on my hair.

CHAPTER 37

THE ONE DRAYKIS, OR WHATEVER type of evil it was called, released me as the other watched me rise to my feet.

"So, are you monsters going to teach me a lesson?" I said, woozy.

Both were taller than me, framed like big men, coated in assorted dragon scales. One smiled, showing an extra row of teeth as it continued to smack its man's fist into its hand. The other wasn't much different, aside from two horns, and both wore a mish-mash of metal armor. I couldn't imagine what they needed that for. Their eyes were bright yellow dots of evil that glowered at me like a last meal.

"Aren't you going to introduce yourselves?"

Circling me, both creatures howled and gnashed their teeth, their bare arms grasping the air.

One said, "Pain."

The other said, "Destruction."

"You," one said in a growl as it waved me forward, "come fight. Come."

"So many words you know; good for you. I imagine that's no small chore with all those rotten teeth in your mouth." I stepped up, squared up, and raised my fists at it approached.

It chuckled.

"Have it your way then," I said, jabbing my hand into its rock-hard chin.

I danced back, shaking my human hand. Now my hand would be as swollen as my face.

"Use your other arm, Idiot! Sultans of Sulfur!"

I ducked under one blow and sidestepped another. It was fast, but I was faster. I launched my dragon fist into its face, rocking its head back with a smack.

It staggered back, hissing and shaking its head, eyes narrowing.

"Rooooar!"

The other came, hard and fast, almost bowling me over as I leapt over the top of it.

"You're fast for such a big and ugly thing. I'm impressed, but I can do this all day."

No, I couldn't do it all day. My body felt like it had been shot out of a catapult, and my strength was fading.

Roaring, they both charged again. I swept the

legs out from under one and kicked the other in the gut, doubling it over. Shrugging off my blows, they snarled.

Great! Every monster, no matter how big or strong, has a weak spot. I just had to find it before they found mine—which was probably any place on my body right then.

I caught the charging draykis by its horn, swung onto its back, and slugged it in the ear. It shook its head like an angry bull. Like a gorilla, the other one pounced on my back and dragged me to the ground. I rammed my knee in its ribs. I drove my boot heel in its crotch. Nothing. And that move almost always worked.

"Sultans of Sulfur! What are you things made of!"

The draykis tore into me, claws tearing into my legs and arms, shredding my clothes until I could see my blood dripping on the stone floor. Quicker, I wrestled out from underneath it and made a dash for the wall. Chest heaving, I stuck my arm out and said, "A moment... *gasp*... Please."

Dragons are fast, and these dragon abominations were fast as well. I could outsmart them or out-quick them, but I didn't have anywhere to go. It was like two big cats chasing a bird in a cage. Scanning the room, I saw no other doors or windows. Just columns, stone benches and ancient symbols. *Drat!* I needed another plan. Fast.

Find a weakness. Save the dragons!

Catching my breath, I stepped out from behind the column. The two monsters stood tall, mouths snapping, claws bared, dripping my blood. They were fiends. Men turned into monsters against their wills. Like me. My arm, I saw, wasn't so much different than theirs. But, mine was perfect: black and shiny, a glorious work of art. Their scales were drab. They, unlike me, were monsters. Stone-cold killers. Heartless and cruel. I hated evil! A cauldron erupted inside me. A flood of energy came as I charged.

I struck like a viper—*pow!*—driving my fist into the nearest draykis's jaw. It wobbled on its knees.

"I AM!"

I dunked under the other's fist and shoved my elbow into its ribs. *Crack!*

"NOT!"

Like a tornado, I hit them with everything I could.

Whap! Whap! Whap! Pow! Pow! Pow! Boom!

"A DEMON!"

One fell face first to the mosaic floor.

"A FIEND!"

I hoisted the other one over my head and slammed him through a stone bench.

"OR A MONSTER LIKE YOU!"

Neither draykis moved while I fell to my knees, clutching my sides, shaking. *I did it. I defeated them, but now what?* I was still trapped.

226

"Impossible!" Somewhere, Finnius raged, his voice echoing throughout the chamber.

I brushed my hair from my eyes and spit the taste of blood and dirt from my mouth.

"Where are you, Worm?"

Stone scraped against stone somewhere as a secret passage opened.

"Come, Nath Dragon. You've earned the right to live," Finnius said from somewhere beyond, "but I'm not sure about your friend."

I dashed into the tunnel as I heard the voice of a man, screaming.

"Ben!"

CHAPTER
38

I NSIDE HIS CAGE, THE MALE pixlyn fought against the bars. His mate sang encouraging words that filled him with power. With him straining, the bars began to bend. Exhausted, the pixlyn squeezed free. He flew over and grabbed a ring of keys that hung from a peg on the wall. Seconds later, he unlocked his mate's cage, and they were free. Tossing the keys on the floor, neither looked back, and they were gone. From a lone cage in the corner, a little white dragon saw it all.

The temple was a series of catacombs that wound from one room or corridor to the next. I passed shelves, tombs, and altars but nothing undead. In pain, I trudged forward as fast as I could, worried, exhausted.

"Nath!" a voice cried from out of nowhere. Stopping, I turned and saw a familiar face in an ancient mirror bigger than me. It was Ben, bleeding and beaten. "Help me, Nath!"

All my hairs stood up on end as the haunting voice faded and the image disappeared.

I stood staring at the mirror and gawped at myself. I'd never looked so bad before. My face was swollen, my nose broken, and my ribs felt like scattered pieces from a dwarven puzzle. "Ben," I muttered, touching the glass. I had to save him. I had to find him fast.

I turned my back to the mirror and yelled.
"Enough, Finnius Worm, show yourself!"
Nothing.

I decided to renew my search, and I was heading toward another tunnel when I heard Finnius say, "So close yet so far, Fool."

Now Finnius's image was inside the large oval mirror, taunting me, mocking me. "You'll never find your friend in time, but I thank you. He'll make a fine meal for the draykis. Even monsters get hungry."

Finnius's words went straight through me.
"Noooooo!"

I charged across the chamber in two leaps, lowering my shoulder as I crashed through the mirror.

Glass shattered as I passed from one side to the other and kept going. Fear assailed me. I spiraled downward, free falling through the darkness before hitting the hard ground with a thud. I could have sworn I broke every bone in my body when I tried to rise to my feet.

"Welcome, Nath Dragon. How fine of you it was to join us."

Finnius stood on the other side of thick metal bars, gloating.

"My, I never imagined you would have fallen for that one. You actually ran through the mirror and fell into the pit. It's one of the stupidest things I've ever seen. And coming from you, Nath Dragon, one of the greatest warriors of all. Tsk. Tsk. I can't begin to express how disappointed and elated I am." He drummed his chin with his fingers. "Then again, maybe I'm just, oh, I almost hate to say it... Brilliant!"

My prison was solid steel, corroded, but solid nonetheless. High above me, a trap door was being pulled up and into place. I wasn't going anywhere, not without help.

"Where's Ben?"

"Oh, the young man whom you have doomed? Why, he's over there, dying," Finnius said, pointing.

I felt my heart stop in my chest. Ben spun in midair, surrounded by acolytes muttering a spell. Ben's eyes were watery with terror as his unmoving lips seemed to cry out for me. We locked eyes, but he couldn't even blink.

"What are you doing to him, Finnius!" I shouted through the bars.

Finnius lifted his finger up and said, "Ah, well you are going to like this, really. You see, when the High Priestess arrives, she is going to teach me how to create a draykis. You see Nath, all we have to do is add dragon parts." He pointed farther back in the room. "And dragon blood."

I could see several cages with coiled up dragons inside. One was a yellow streak, the other two evergreens inside eerie glowing cages.

"That's not going to happen, Worm. I'll see to that."

Finnius let out a creepy bubbly laugh as he walked over and grabbed my sword from one of his acolytes.

"I wouldn't draw that blade, if I were you."

"What is the matter, Dragon? Are you afraid I'll kill you with it?"

"It doesn't like evil," I said, pulling myself up by the bars. "You'd best let go of that."

"Hah. Nice try, Dragon. But, I believe I'll be alright. Oh, and don't worry: as I said, I'm not going to kill you. The High Priestess will do that. But, I will at some point, have to kill your young friend, Ben. And won't it be agonizing to watch him die by your own blade? Hmmmm?"

231

"He dies, you die, Worm."

Holding Fang by the scabbard, Finnius eyed me then the sword and said, "Acolyte, withdraw this blade."

"Again, Finnius, I wouldn't do that unless you want another man dead," I warned.

The acolyte's fingers stopped inches from Fang's hilt. He widened his eyes on me.

"Withdraw it, Servant, or die anyway! Draykis!"

Several hulking figures stepped out of the shadows, two of which limped and had busted faces. It seemed all of my valiant efforts from earlier had been deflated. One stepped over the acolyte and wrapped its clawed fingers around his neck.

Sweating profusely, the acolyte wrapped his trembling hands around the hilt. Taking a sharp breath, he slid Fang out from the sheath, holding my sword out in his robed arms. Fang's steel flickered with life in the lantern light, but was otherwise dim. I sagged. I hadn't really expected Fang to do anything, but you never know with him.

"Huh, I see your bluff has failed you, Dragon. Perhaps you should have stayed in bed. You look awfully tired. Maybe you should just sit down and rest." Finnius jerked the sword away from the acolyte and pointed it in the acolyte's face. He clipped one cheek, then the other. "Next time, it will be your neck with a large hole in it." Finnius whirled towards the others and said, "Lower him."

Ben's body slowly drifted over next to a large stone altar, where he sat upright, listless and catatonic. They had done something to him. His eyes flickered between me, the draykis and the ceiling.

"Don't give up, Ben. I'll save you!"

"No Dragon, no you won't," Finnius said, stepping over towards Ben and stabbing him in the chest.

"NOOOOOOOOOOOOO!"

CHAPTER

39

I DIDN'T FEEL A THING WHEN my buttocks landed on the cold stone floor. I was dead inside. Worse, Ben was dead! The only thought racing through my head was, 'It's your life to throw away, not mine.' I'd tried to warn him, yet guilt overwhelmed me. It mixed with something else: anger. It was all my fault. I had failed.

"Good, Dragon," Finnius started, "you should rest as you look absolutely horrible. I hope the High Priestess doesn't mind when she arrives any minute now." He clapped his hands. "Acolytes, begin the summons."

Listless, I watched the Clerics of Barnabus gather around an archway off center in the chamber and begin their moans and mumbles. I felt my heart explode in my chest when the draykis hoisted Ben's body up onto the slab altar.

"I'll kill you, Finnius," I muttered.

Finnius cupped his ear, saying, "What's that?" He jabbed Fang into the stone floor by the altar. "A fine weapon, a fine-fine piece of steel. Is it made of Jaxite? I didn't even feel it go in or slide out." He turned his attention to the archway and looked back at me. "Won't be long now, Dragon. And I can't wait to see what the High Priestess has in store for you."

Smoke of many colors swirled inside the archway, pulsating with life and energy. The sound of the acolytes chanting increased in volume and tempo. I didn't care. Whoever the High Priestess was and whatever they wanted to do with me didn't matter. I'd failed. I'd abandoned one friend, only to see another one dead. Huffing for air, I rose to my feet. I wrapped my hands around the metal.

"I'm going to kill you, Finnius!"

I wasn't supposed to kill anybody, unless it was life or death. *What about Finnius's death for Ben's life?* It was more than fair.

Finnius leered at me, wringing his dirty hands together and saying, "Not even in your wildest nightmares. It's over for you, Nath Dragon."

The draykis, no longer two but ten, sprang into action as something small and white skittered across the floor.

"What is it!" Finnius cried out as a small white dragon leaped past his face and into the corner.

"Who let it out! I'll kill one of you! Acolyte, get me those Pixlyn!" One broke from the group and dashed off. "Draykis, capture that dragon!"

It was a long-tailed white, the same one I'd seen in the cage on my way in here. Quick and fierce, the draykis were no match for it. One sealed off the other way out as the other three chased it around the room. It scurried, hissed, snapped and slipped through the claws of one then the other.

"Get it, Draykis! Kill it!" Finnius screamed. "It doesn't matter how!"

I jumped to my feet, pulling at the bars, fuming.

"I'll not see any more of your murders, Finnius.

"You'll see many more before this day is over, I assure you."

The acolyte rushed back into the room.

"Well?" Finnius snapped.

"Gone, Cleric Finnius."

Finnius wrung his hands and tugged at his robes, screaming at the draykis, "You idiots! Why did you abandon those cages!"

The draykis at the door replied, "We did as you requested."

The long-tailed white flew from one side of the room to the other.

Finnius stomped his feet.

"Catch it! NOW!"

The long-tailed white locked eyes with me, and I felt a connection. It wanted the dragons free, and so did I.

Finnius howled. He saw us.

The dragon darted across the room towards me.

"Stop it!" Finnius yelled.

Lunging, two draykis collided with each other, but a third caught the end of the dragon's long tail and jerked it to the ground. The dragon screeched, tiny claws digging into the stone floor, straining towards me. I reached through the bars, my arm inches away.

"NO!" I screamed as another draykis, wielding a sword, rushed over, swinging it.

"Kill it!" Finnius shouted. "Kill it!"

CHAPTER
40

T HE WHITE DRAGON'S EYES GLOWED with green
fire as the draykis swung the sword. A jet of
white smoke shot out of its mouth, filling
the room in an instant. I couldn't see a thing, but
I heard a blade chopping into flesh and stone.
Something let out a nasty grunt, and I could hear
Finnius hack and cough while I tried to fan the
smoke away. As the smoke dissipated, I could hear
him scream.

"Did you kill it? Where is it? Find it!"

Through the thinning smoke, a draykis rose
from the floor, staring at the stump of his arm.
The other with the sword was looking around, and
that's when I felt it. The tiny dragon had squeezed
through the bars and was crawling up my back and
onto my shoulder. His extra-long tail coiled along
my waist and arm.

"Ahem," I said.

Finnius turned my way. His face reddened and his chin quivered when he said, "Give me that long-tailed white, Dragon. Or I'll kill the rest of them."

"If you want this dragon, Worm, why don't you come and get it?"

The dragon's tail tightened around my arm and waist. A surge of power raced through me like never before. Every muscle in my being pulsated as the purring dragon filled me with awesome power. I wasn't a man any more. I felt the strength of a full-grown dragon. I grabbed the bars, and the metal groaned as I pulled them apart like noodles. Finnius's jaw dropped to the floor when I stepped through the gap I'd just made.

"Unless you can bring my friend back to life, it's time to die, Finnius!"

I knocked the first draykis that came at me from one side of the room to the other. I ducked under another blade that almost took my head from my shoulders. I was fast. Faster than ever before. Stronger than ever before. The power the little dragon gave me was unbelievable!

"You're dead!" I said, rushing Finnius.

He had turned to run before I closed in when two armed draykis jumped into my path. A sharp blade tore past my stomach, and a large hammer ripped an inch away from my head. I was faster and stronger, but I wasn't impervious to metal. I did a back flip towards the altar and landed in front of Fang. I ripped him free.

"Now it's even, uglies," I said. I could feel the dragon's power flowing from my shins to my neck. Fang's blade hummed with life. "Who's the first to pay for the life of my friend!"

"You cannot kill us," said one draykis, holding a sword. "We are already dead."

"We'll see about that," I boasted, knowing full well the odds were against me. I'd never faced such a formidable force of warriors before. So be it. I felt like I could fight an entire army now. I felt even better than when the crowd had cheered me on, "Dragon! Dragon!"

Faster than sight, I drove Fang into the nearest one's chest, drawing forth a groan as it fell. I chopped another one in the arm and kicked another one in the face. Another parried my strike and countered with a deep cut across my leg. On they came at me with the skill and precision of hardened soldiers, forcing me backward to parry again and again.

"NO!"

I knocked a blade free from one and stabbed another in the shoulder. Another fell as I hacked through its knee. Fang cut through the air like a living thing. Cutting, blocking, and chopping. But all my strength and speed didn't stop them from coming. Limping, snarling, and slashing, they pressed.

"Gah!"

One ripped its claws through my arm. Little dragon or not, I couldn't keep this up much longer, and if I died, the dragons would all die as well.

Without thinking, I said, "Fang! Do something!"

Fang flared with brilliant icy light.

Striking like a snake, I jabbed a draykis that wielded a sword.

It stopped in its tracks, its scaled body turned to ice. I struck another draykis and one more. Instant statues of ice they'd become. I cut one in the arm and another in the leg with the same effect. Weapons poised high over their heads, the last two charged.

Slice! Slice!

They crystalized into pure ice.

There I stood among eight frozen horrors, feeling almost as astounded as they looked. Fang throbbed in my hand.

"What's that, Fang?" I saw the tip flare up. "Ah, I see."

I struck Fang's tip on the stone floor.

KRAAAAAAAAAAAANG!

The perfect metal resonated through the chamber like a giant tuning fork.

One by one, the icy figures of the draykis exploded into a thousand shards of ice.

241

"NOOOOOOOOOOOOOO!" Finnius screamed from right behind me.

I whirled just in time to catch a long dagger plunging at my chest. I twisted it free from his wrist, punched him in the face, and sent him sprawling to the floor.

"You're going to pay, Worm!"

Crawling backward, he shouted back, "It's too late, Dragon. She comes."

The mystic smoke in the archway was filling the room, but all the clerics but Finnius were gone. Eeriness covered me like a blanket. I shook it off.

"Great, then she'll be here just in time to make arrangements for your funeral." I raised my sword and closed in. I didn't ever want to see this man alive again. "But there might not be much left to bury once I'm done with you."

"Go ahead! Kill me! My High Priestess will just bring me back," Finnius said, chuckling. "But that's much more than I can say for your friend." His eyes twinkled with darkness as his lips curled in a smile. "Come Dragon, Avenge your friend."

"I'll do more than that!"

The dragon on my shoulder hissed out a warning.

Crack!

It felt like a large mallet collided with my skull, knocking me to my knees. Finnius seized my wrists and shouted.

"AZZRHEEM-KAH!

It felt like lightning exploded inside me as I lay on the ground, hair smoking, every fiber of my being throbbing in pain. My eyelids hurt as I opened my eyes to witness a winged draykis reaching for me. Bigger than the rest, it scooped me off the floor like a doll and crushed me in its arms.

"Break his back!" Finnius yelled from somewhere. "I want to hear it snap, Draykis!"

It didn't have lips, but it smiled.

"Certainly, my Lord."

CHAPTER

41

ALL MY STRENGTH FLED WHEN I gazed at the small white dragon lying still on the floor. Completely drained, I fought on, legs kicking, but the monster had its mighty paws locked behind my back.

"That's it!" Finnius said with glee. "Ooh! Your face is awfully red, Dragon, but I think it will look even better in a nice dark shade of purple." Finnius limped over, leering up at me, triumphant.

I felt it. I was defeated. I'd failed. Any moment, the winged draykis would crush all my bones, leaving me living but an invalid.

"Worm!" I managed to spit out.

My spit sizzled through his robes.

"Eh... What is this?" Finnius asked, fingering the hole in his robes. My stomach churned with fire, and the taste of brimstone charged inside my mouth.

The draykis licked its lips, said, "I'm hungry," and squeezed me with all its might.

I felt something snap as hot smoke burst from my nose.

Eyes filled with horror, Finnius backed away. "NO! What are you doing, Dragon? Stop that! Make him stop, Draykis. NOW!"

The draykis, jaws filled with long sharp teeth, opened wide.

I tried to scream, but a jet of flaming hot liquid erupted instead.

One second the draykis's horrible face was about to eat me, in the next it was a ball of fire. There was nothing left of its face but bone as it released me and fell to the ground.

I jumped up from the floor to chase Finnius down.

He slipped on the shards of ice and fell hard to the ground on his knees, saying, "Mercy, Dragon! Mercy!"

Evil shows no mercy. No mercy shall it receive.

"Where was your mercy when you killed my friend, Worm?"

"Mercy! I'll do anything! Please!"

I wanted to stop it, but I couldn't. A geyser of flame shot from my mouth, coating Finnius from head to toe. In an instant, he was burnt to a crisp.

A new rush of power assailed me as I chased the other acolytes down. Some burned, some escaped, and some died before it was over.

The only ones left were me and the dragons. One by one, I freed them from their cages, and one by one they were gone. The long-tailed white as well. Exhausted, I fell to my knees and fought the tears coming from my eyes.

"Ben," I moaned as I crawled over to the altar.

There he lay on the granite slab altar, pale as a ghost. His energetic face, once full of life, now as stiff as stone. I'd saved the dragons but at what cost?

I brushed the hair from his eyes and said, "Ben. I'm so sorry, Ben."

"For what?" he said, blinking.

I stiffened.

"Huh? Ben?"

He yawned, stretched out his arms and asked again, "For what?"

I stumbled backward, clutching my heart.

"BEN! You're alive!"

"That seems to be the case," he said, fanning the eerie smoke from his face. "Is that your breath that I smell? It's awful."

"I guess that's why they call it dragon breath."

Sitting on the altar, Ben said, "Is this place shaking?"

Shards of rock and debris fell on my head and

his. The High Priestess. Was she still coming? I rushed over and grabbed Fang. But where was Akron—and the rest of my things?

"We need to get out of here, Ben."

Something was coming through the portal, something big.

"Ben, do you see my bow?"

I swung Fang into the archway, splintering rock, but it held. I felt the urge to hew the thing down. I felt evil as great as I'd ever felt before.

"Found it!" Ben said, hoisting it over his head.

"Bring it over here."

I snatched Akron from his hands and nocked it with a powerful arrow. I rubbed my spit in the tip and watched it glow.

Holding his ears, Ben shouted, "What are you doing?"

"I don't know," I said as I let the arrow fly. It disappeared into the smoky archway. A split second later, a roar came out that shook the entire temple. I grabbed Ben by the arm and led us dashing through the corridors. The floors wobbled and the walls warbled as we rushed past the dust and debris through one winding corridor and another until we arrived outside in the courtyard. The night air was like ice in my breath.

"We made it," I said, leaning over and grabbing my knees.

Ben was lying on the courtyard grass, wheezing.

From inside the ruins of the temple came a mighty thud like someone closing the lid on a giant sarcophagus. I fell to my knees, rain pelting my face, and scanned the area. No acolytes, lizardmen or draykis. It was over.

For a moment, I took it all in. I was alive, but more importantly so was Ben.

"Look," Ben said pointing.

A group of small dragons flew across the moonlit clouds in the sky.

I wanted to hug Ben but didn't. Smiling, I squeezed his shoulder instead and said, "Ben, why aren't you dead?"

He shrugged.

"I think Bayzog's potion did it."

"How so?"

"Well, he said that I would know when it was time to take it, so I did."

"And when was that?"

"Well, I was with the horses, like you said, guarding them like you told me. After you'd been gone a little while, the horses started whining."

"Whining?"

"Yes, I've never seen such nervous horses before. And that's when I noticed it." He stopped, thinking.

"Noticed what?"

"A giant shadow circling in the sky." He shivered. "I'd never been so scared in all of my life. And I knew, instantly, that it was coming for me. That thing, those eyes, locked on mine, and I knew I was dead. I grabbed that vial and swallowed the entire bottle full. The horses galloped off, and the next thing I knew I was face to face with it. I'm embarrassed, but I think I fainted in its arms. I awoke, and I was sailing across the sky like a bird. That monster was carrying me. That's when I blacked out again. Next time I awoke, I was spinning in that room, surrounded by those clerics and beastly things. Then that man took your sword and stabbed me."

He pulled off his leather armor, which was cut clean through. He ran his finger along the white scar on his chest. He shook his head. "It was cold, the blade going in. As if someone shoved ice in my chest. But I didn't die; I felt strange, outside of myself. I just closed my eyes and played possum." He put his armor back on. "What was in that vial, Dragon?"

"Let's get out of here," I said, grimacing.

I headed for the forest—limping, bleeding and aching all over. I'd had enough of these temples.

"Well, what was it?"

"I can't say for sure, because you can never tell with Bayzog, or any other wizard, for that matter, but I'd say what he gave you was Moments of Immortality. And that's very potent magic."

"Whoa... How many moments do you think I have?"

I socked him in the arm.

"Ow! Why'd you do that?"

"Do you feel Immortal?"

"No," he said, rubbing his arm.

"Then I'd say your moments ran out. Now come on: maybe we can track down the horses by dawn if we run."

"Run?"

I took off, but not as fast as I would have liked. My joints ached. My body was swollen like a watered down log. I'd taken a pretty heavy beating those last couple of days. But Ben, despite his huffing, tried to keep up. I had to let him catch up.

"There should be a potion to make this running easier," he wheezed.

"There is. Come on."

We arrived back at the Crane's Neck as dawn broke and began the search for the horses. Starting from where Ben left them, I spotted the hoof prints in the dirt.

Kneeling down and pointing, I said, "See these horseshoe prints, Ben? They left deep impressions after the rain, so they shouldn't be hard to follow—unless another storm hits. And they won't take off more than a mile. With any luck, they're grazing somewhere. Why don't you see if you can track them?"

His face lit up.

"Really, me?"

"Now's as good a time to practice as any."

"Alright then," he replied, giving me a funny look. "Well, uh, Dragon, do you feel alright?"

"I'm fine. I've been in plenty of bad scrapes before. Why do aaaaa—?"

I forgot what I was saying. My lids became heavy as Ben's eyes filled with alarm. His mouth twisted like a pinwheel as he yelled, and his fingers stretched out like worms. *What's happening?* The light of the dawn faded to black.

Inside the temple ruins, a magnificent woman surveyed the chamber where the battle had taken place. It was High Priestess Selena.

"Interesting."

Hours earlier, she had been attempting to enter the portal when a magic arrow sailed through the smoke, struck a draykis, and blew it and another to pieces. Her chamber room was half destroyed, and her roar wiped out most of what wasn't already. She'd gotten over it. Not all plans were perfectly executed, but the execution still had its rewards.

She stepped through a puddle of water, kneeled along the charred corpse of Finnius, and said, "The best pawns end up being dead pawns." She grabbed the magic amulet from around his neck and pulled it free of his charred remains. "Here," she said, tossing it to a man among the draykis. He was big and armored, with many colorful tattoos on his head. A cruel looking warrior's mace hung from his belt.

"Clearly, this was a job for a High Cleric, but..." She waded past the other burnt and broken bodies in the room. "I still think it will bear the results that I was hoping for. Humph. Nath Dragon evades traps with the cunning of a snake, but he'll never escape the biggest trap of all."

"And that is?" the deep voiced warrior cleric said.

"Himself."

Before she stepped through the smoke in the archway, she commanded one more thing.

"And bring along all the corpses of the acolytes. The dead tell the most accurate tales."

CHRONICLES OF DRAGON

Clutch of the Cleric

CHAPTER 1

I FELT LIKE I'D GONE DAYS without water when I opened my eyes up. A soft soothing light was in my eyes, but I still felt weary.

"Uh... where am I? Ben?"

The smell of sweet ginger filled my nostrils, and someone placed a cold damp cloth on my head.

"Sssssh. Rest, Dragon."

The warm face of Sasha greeted me with a smile as she reached over and touched my face.

"Bayzog, he awakens again."

Again? I didn't remember waking the last time.

"It's not time yet, Sasha," Bayzog said. A faint image of him in his red wizard tunic caught my eye.

Her perfect lips started singing; the gentle, mystic words of an ancient lullaby churned in my ears.

"No, don't do thaaaaaa—"

The soft lights turned dark again.

"Wake him up!"

Slowly, I opened my eyes, the thirst I remembered now gone. Then I saw Brenwar, as angry as I ever saw him before.

"What are you yelling for?" I said, shielding my eyes, squinting.

He whirled on me, so angry I could see the red behind his beard.

"WHAT AM I YELLING FOR?"

A large figure stepped between us. It was one of those Roaming Rangers.

"Shum?"

"Get out of my way, Elf," Brenwar growled.

"Brenwar," Bayzog intervened, "now is not the time."

"Oh, it's the time, alright!"

Brenwar shoved past Shum, stuck his stubby finger in my face, and said, "Why did you leave me, Nath Dragon!" His voice cracked. "Why did you do that?"

I didn't know what to say. I was feeling great, but I had the feeling I shouldn't be.

"Why is everyone looking at me like that?

Where's Ben? Is he alright? And how did I get here?"

Brenwar stood frowning and tapping his foot, Shum unmoving, Bayzog muttering and Sasha twitching her nose.

"What?" I said.

Bayzog took a seat beside me and said, "I'll catch you up. Ben led you back here on the horses after you fainted."

"Ah good, I knew Ben had it in him. I guess my wounds were much worse than I thought. So, where is he?"

"He's with the Legionnaires, on a mission."

"Huh, a mission. He couldn't be on a mission already. Could he? Don't they have to go through training?"

Brenwar stormed forward.

"Fool! He could have been on twenty missions already. He's been gone for weeks. You've been asleep for weeks. I've been looking for you; my men have been looking for you, and we might never have found you if we hadn't come across that temple. And we might not have ever known you were there if we hadn't found this!" He held out a black dragon scale. "And this led us here."

I grabbed the scale with my left hand and pinched it in my fingers. My black dragon fingers. I jumped off the couch.

"SULTANS OF SULFUR! I have two dragon arms!"

"You can say that again!" Brenwar shot back. "You foolish dragon!"

I touched my toes, my shins, my thighs, chest and face.

"Am I?"

"Just the arms, Dragon," Sasha said. "You'll be alright."

"No, he won't! He'd have been alright if he'd done as he was told. Dragon! What have you done?" Brenwar exclaimed.

"I saved dragons!" I yelled back. "And if I'd waited on you, they'd probably be dead!"

I gazed at my scales, my hands, my claws. A thrill went through me. I felt unstoppable! But there was something else. The white spot of scales was on both palms in the middle.

Brenwar poked me in the chest, saying, "I was at the temple. I saw what you did. And your new friend, Ben, confirmed it. You killed again! Now look at you!"

"You started it!" I said, pointing at Brenwar.

"You did this, not I, Dragon! You ran off on your own, like a fool, and now you have twice the problem!"

"Don't call me a Fool again, Brenwar," I said, glowering down on him. I was ready to rip his beard off.

He rose up on his toes and said, "What are you going to do, breathe on me? Fool!"

I took a deep breath.

He laughed at me.

Sasha's vibrant form stepped between us. "Please, everyone, stop yelling. You aren't children; you're men," Sasha said, gentle hands pushing me into the sofa.

Calmness fell over me.

"We have to work together on this." She said, eyeing all of us. "It's that important. Bayzog, tell him."

I slumped into the sofa, feeling incredibly angry and guilty, but I let Sasha's charm calm me.

"Yes, Bayzog, Ben mentioned there was something you wanted to tell me. What is it?" I said, noticing my beard. "Ugh! Really?"

Bayzog gave me a funny look.

I shook my head, which was beginning to ache, saying, "Go on then."

"Dragon, I can't say that I, or anyone in the world, for that matter, can understand your unique constitution—well, excluding your father, of course."

My head started aching. What would my father think?

"I don't think things are as bad as they look, however. I would venture that it was inevitable that you would start turning into a dragon eventually, and your scales, well, they aren't a true reflection of your nature. Nath, we all know that you are good, as good a man as we all know, but there is darkness in all of us. No one person is perfect or without blemish; most just hide it better on the outside. That's why it is difficult to tell the good people from the evil sometimes."

"This isn't helping, Bayzog," I said, holding my head in my hands, irritated.

"Our deeds are what define us. Our actions. Our words. Not our garments, not our looks. What is inside a man, in his heart—his dragon heart—is what counts. Keep doing what you are doing."

"But I want to get rid of it." *Sort of.*

"And what if you can't? Will you stop being good altogether then? Will you join the Clerics of Barnabus?"

"NO!"

"So stop whining then," Bayzog said.

"I'm not whining."

"You are whining," Brenwar added, folding his arms across his chest. "Like a baby orc."

"Fine, I'm whining, but I'm sure all of you would do the same if you had these." I lifted my arms. "I'm not going to be wooing the ladies like I used to; that's for sure. But, I imagine I could be used in a carnival to frighten children."

Brenwar harrumphed.

"I like them," Sasha said, rubbing my scales, smiling. "I think they are marvelous."

Her sweet words made me feel better; they really did. I guess I was just going to have to get used it, but I really needed to fix it.

"Bayzog, my father says there are many things in this world that can heal. Perhaps you can help me find some of those things. Maybe I just need a different Thunderstone or something."

Bayzog walked over to his large table, opened his tome, thumbed through the pages, and threw his hands out. When he twitched his fingers, an image of a mystic amulet formed and hung in the air, gold and silver with a bright green gemstone in the middle.

"The Ocular of Orray. The legend says that it can bring health, peace and prosperity. Its powers have been known to cure lycanthropes and liches, and to restore the undead. Perhaps it can help."

"So, where is it?"

Bayzog flicked his fingers. The amulet broke into several pieces.

"It was stolen from the elves in Elome a century after the last Dragon War, never to be seen again. According to the lore, the thieves broke it up into many pieces and spread them all over Nalzambor, for the Ocular cannot be destroyed."

"So, who stole it? Who can go into Elome and steal anything?" Nath sighed. "It's a fortress."

"We'd have to ask the elves that," he said, closing the book.

"So, I'm supposed to search the entire world for this Ocular? I'd rather just save the dragons." I looked at Shum. "And what are you doing here?"

"I have an interest in the power of the Ocular as well. Remember my King? He needs the healing, too."

"I see. And what about the dragons? I'm not going to abandon them for this quest."

Brenwar shoved my sword and scabbard in my chest.

"We won't!"

Bayzog and Sasha donned their traveling cloaks.

"Where are you going?"

"With you," Sasha said, tying the neck with the magic of her fingers. "I've been needing to stretch my legs. Bayzog has kept me cooped up in here too long."

It seemed everybody was ready for a trip but me as I shook my head and rose to my feet.

"So, now I need supervision everywhere I go?"

"And then some," Brenwar huffed. "Let's go!"

"Fine," I said, buckling my sword around my waist as Sasha draped my quiver over my shoulder and handed me Akron. I was ready for anything. But before I closed my eyes, I said one last thing. "But I'm going to save whoever and whatever I want to. Agreed?"

Everyone shook their heads except Brenwar, who laughed.

"Well, let it never be said I didn't consort with highly unreasonable people."

As soon as I closed my eyes, the adventure began.

ABOUT THE AUTHOR

Craig Halloran resides with his family outside of his hometown of Charleston, West Virginia. When he isn't entertaining mankind, he is seeking adventure, working out, or watching sports. To learn more about him, go to: www.thedarkslayer. com

WORKS BY THE AUTHOR

THE DARKSLAYER: SERIES 1
Wrath of the Royals (Book 1)
Blades in the Night (Book 2)
Underling Revenge (Book 3)
Danger and the Druid (Book 4)
Outrage in the Outlands (Book 5)
Chaos at the Castle (Book 6)

THE DARKSLAYER: SERIES 2
Bish and Bone
Black Blood
Red Death

THE CHRONICLES OF DRAGON
The Hero, The Sword and The dragons (Book 1)
Dragon Bones and Tombstones (Book 2)
Terror at the Temple (Book 3)
Clutch of the Cleric (Book 4)
Hunt for the Hero (Book 5)
Settlements under Siege (Book 6)
Strife in the Sky (Book 7)

ZOMBIE IMPACT: SERIES 1
Zombie Day Care: Book 1
Zombie Rehab: Book 2
Zombie Warfare: Book 3

Connect with him at:
Facebook – The Darkslayer Report by Craig
Twitter – Craig Halloran

Made in the USA
San Bernardino, CA
10 January 2016